ASKING
FOR
TROUBLE

Also by Sarah Prineas

ASKING FOR TROUBLE

Sarah Prineas

VIKING

VIKING

An imprint of Penguin Random House LLC, New York

First published in the United States of America by Viking,
an imprint of Penguin Random House LLC, 2022

Copyright © 2022 by Sarah Prineas

Viking & colophon are registered trademarks of Penguin Random House LLC.

Visit us online at penguinrandomhouse.com.

Library of Congress Cataloging-in-Publication Data is available.

Manufactured in Canada

ISBN 9780593204306

1 3 5 7 9 10 8 6 4 2

FRI

Edited by Kelsey Murphy

Design by Monique Sterling

Text set in Plantin

To my BFFs

Jenn Reese, Deb Coates, and Greg van Eekhout

You know what a black hole is, right? It's what happens when a star dies.

Yep, as a star is dying, it collapses in on itself until all its atoms are squished into this teeny space, and then its intense gravity warps the fabric of space-time and starts sucking in everything around it. I mean *everything*. Planets, other stars, even light particles. It all gets gobbled up. Nothing escapes from a black hole. It's a huge, hungry beast.

There are dead stars—black holes—wandering around all over our galaxy.

And at the very center of our galaxy lurks the biggest one—a super-massive black hole.

Don't worry. The black hole at our galactic center is not going to gobble up our entire galaxy. It's big, but our galaxy is way bigger. It's more like . . . a donut.

Just in case you don't know what a donut is, it's a human food that is like a round cake with a hole in the middle. It might be the best food in the entire universe, especially sprinkled with powdered sugar. Mmmm.

Our galaxy is like a 587,900,000,000,000,000-mile-wide

donut, except the hole in the middle is a black hole, and compared to the size of the donut, it's tiny.

Sweeping out from the edges of the black hole is the rest
of the galaxy, crowded with 400 billion stars and even more
planets and comets and asteroids and other black holes, and
clouds of dust and gas. There's trade and space stations, and
shopping moons, and spaceships, and light and color and lots
of different kinds of people, and the StarLeague keeping it all
in order.

But if you keep going, away from the black-hole galactic
center, away from the swirls of stars and planets, you get to the
edge of the galaxy. The Deep Dark. This far out, the stars are
faint pinpoints and you can almost go off the edge, out into
nothing but nothingness, forever.

1

"We," Captain Astra announces, "have just encountered something interesting."

I know my captain. When she says *interesting*, it doesn't mean what you think it does.

We're in the mess-room of the spaceship *Hindsight*. The mess-room is the bright, colorful place where the crew gets together to eat, and also to socialize, and for important meetings, which is what this is.

At the head of the long table is the captain, who's leaning back in her chair with both hands behind her head. She has light brown skin, curly white-gray hair, and brown eyes with wrinkles at the corners. Right now her wrinkles are crinkled because she's smiling widely at the rest of us. "*Very* interesting," she repeats.

Next to her is Electra Zox, my best friend. As usual, she

is tense, her hands clenched, her green skin a little pale, and her tintacles are dark gray. Tintacles are kind of like hair, but more tentacly, and they change color depending on how she's feeling. Dark gray means that she's suspicious.

Then comes Telly, our vegetarian cargo master, who is grinning around his tusks. "What're you planning?" he asks Captain Astra.

"Oh, you're going to *love* it," she answers. Then she nods at one of the Shkkka, who is standing in the doorway. The Shkkka are three insectoids who are one person, and they are our ship's engineer. "Is the ship ready to go?" the captain asks her. "Because we need to *move*."

The Shkkka twitches her antennae, which means *yes*.

There's one person missing from the crew, and that's Amby, the tall blue humanoid who was our navigator. They returned to their home planet to be with their other family.

Instead of Amby, we have a new navigator. He's a humanoid. He says that his name is impossible for us to pronounce; we call him Fred.

Then comes me. One of two shapeshifters in the entire galaxy. I'm curled in Amby's old nest chair in my human boy shape: pale skin, brown hair, brown eyes. Protein bar wrappers are scattered around me. I am listening to the captain while keeping an eye on the thing sitting on a plate in the middle of the table.

It looks like a delicious donut sprinkled with powdered sugar.

The donut isn't doing anything. It's just sitting there.

At the head of the table, the captain gives a nod toward Reetha, the big green-scaled lizardian who is in charge of our communications and security. "You want to tell them about the interesting thing?" the captain asks. "Or should I?"

Reetha, who doesn't talk much, and also doesn't blink—lizardians don't have eyelids to blink with—just stares back at the captain with her golden, slit-pupilled eyes.

The captain leans forward. "I'll tell them." She rubs her hands together and makes a low laughing sound that is almost a cackle. *Heh-heh-heh.* "Reetha picked up a signal from the edge of the galaxy."

"Deep. Dark," Reetha corrects.

Captain Astra shrugs. "The edge of the Deep Dark, but not actually outside our galaxy." She looks around at all of us. "Reetha detected a strange blip on the sensors. We think it might be a certain lost ship . . ."

Everybody looks blankly back at her.

"A ship packed with supplies," she hints. "Lost, drifting around the galaxy, big news about twelve years ago . . ."

"No." Telly's eyes widen. "Not the *Skeleton?*"

"Hah!" the captain says, and bangs the table with her hand. "Yes. The *Skeleton.*"

I must look blanker than everybody else, because the captain grins at me. "Never heard of the *Skeleton*, Trouble?"

"Nope," I tell her, and take a bite of protein bar.

"Twelve years ago," she explains, "the *Skeleton* was a cargo ship stuffed with valuable supplies on its way from a station near the galactic center to a newly settled planet on the Outer Rim. And then—" She makes a wavy motion with her hands; I think it's supposed to be spooky. "And *then*, it disappeared, like a ghost, never to be heard from again."

"Until now," I say.

"Until now," she confirms.

"If it's been twelve years," I ask, "wouldn't the *Skeleton*'s cargo be rotten or falling apart?"

Telly's the cargo expert. "It'd be in stasis," he tells me. "Perfectly preserved." His furry ears twitch, making the bells on his earrings tinkle.

"Metals and wood," the captain says. "Farming machinery, precious seeds, medical supplies. Treasure!" She gives another cackle, and I remember that she is, at heart, sort of a pirate. "All ours!" She points at our new navigator. "Fred," she orders, "set a new course—for the edge of the Deep Dark. We're going to find the *Skeleton*!"

See? When my captain says *interesting*, what she really means is *dangerous*.

2

On his way out of the mess-room, our new navigator, Fred, pauses to examine the thing on the plate in the middle of the table that looks like a donut.

Fred is a humanoid, but instead of eyes in his head he has eyestalks that can see in every direction. This means he's impossible to sneak up on, and also when he looks at something, he *really* looks at it. His skin is shiny and wet and a muddy gray color. Below his eyestalks he has regular gray hair and ears and a nose, and then a narrow mouth full of tiny, sharp teeth. When he talks, he sounds like he's biting off every word and spitting it out. He has supplemented his short humanoid arms with a set of two more robot arms that he wears on a belt around his waist.

With one eyestalk Fred is examining the donut; the other eyestalk is looking suspiciously at me.

The rest of the crew is heading out of the mess-room,

talking excitedly about the *Skeleton* and what it'll mean for all of us if we can find it. Except for Electra, who seems angry about something and is glaring at the captain.

I climb out of the nest chair and start to collect the protein bar wrappers.

While I'm distracted, Fred reaches out with one of his regular arms, picks up the donut, and sniffs at it.

"I wouldn't try to eat that if I were you," I tell him.

Here is another thing about Fred: when he eats, he can unhinge his jaw so that his mouth becomes huge enough to swallow things whole.

Sometimes I get so hungry that I wish my human shape could do that.

Fred ignores my warning. He sniffs the thing again. Then his mouth gapes open, bristling with sharp teeth.

"Stop!" I shout.

But he shoves the donut in. His mouth snaps shut.

"No!" I gasp. "Don't swallow it!"

The captain and Electra are in the mess-room doorway; they whirl to see what's going on.

Which is when the baby shapeshifter who's been pretending to be a donut decides it doesn't want to be eaten by Fred, and it shifts into something metallic and covered with needle-sharp spines that make Fred spit it out with a loud *bleck!*

By the time the baby shapeshifter lands on the floor, it's shifted again, this time into its blob of goo form. It slinks under the table and pretends to be invisible.

Fred's giant mouth is hanging open, revealing rows and rows of teeth. Carefully, he closes it and glowers at me with both eyestalks. One of his robot arms reaches out, and a metallic finger pokes me in the chest. "I blame *you* for this," he snaps. His other metallic arm points at the baby shapeshifter. "That creature is a menace!" Then he turns and stomps out of the mess-room. When he passes the captain and Electra, he repeats, "A menace!"

He's not entirely wrong.

I crouch down to check on the baby shapeshifter under the table. In its blob of goo form it's about the size of . . . well, of a donut. Its goo is clear and bubbly, and it looks completely innocent.

But it's not.

Why did it take the shape of a donut?

I'll tell you why. I am the ship's galley boy, which means I'm the one who makes all of the food. A few days ago I made something new. Donuts—human dessert food that are like cakes with a hole in the middle. The crew loved them and demanded that I make them again soon.

By pretending to be a donut, the baby shapeshifter was being very tricky. It wanted somebody to pick it up and try to eat it and then get a big, sharp surprise.

"That wasn't very nice," I tell it.

In response, the blob of goo quivers.

"I know," I say. "You're sorry." At least, I *hope* it is sorry.

Captain Astra's boots appear next to me. I look up, and

she's looking down at me with her hands on her hips. "Trouble, Trouble?" she asks.

"Donut," I say, pointing to the baby shapeshifter. Its goo contracts, and then it shifts into the shape of a protein bar. Does it think I'm dumb enough to try to eat it?

The captain crouches so she can peer under the table. "Donut? Is that what you're calling it?"

"Yep," I say. "I want to take good care of it, and be a good big sibling. But it's harder than I thought it would be."

"Ah." She nods wisely as we get to our feet. "Families. Always complicated." She fixes me with a keen look. "We need Fred. He's one of the best navigators in the galaxy."

Electra is leaning against the wall by the door. "We *know*," she puts in. "He's told us that about fourteen times." She sighs. "I wish Amby hadn't left."

"Thinking about Amby makes me hungry," I say.

"*What?*" Electra says, staring at me.

I pat my stomach. "In here. A sort of hollow feeling. Hungry."

"No, Trouble," Captain Astra corrects. "There's a place where Amby used to be, and now they're gone. You *miss* them. That's the feeling. It's not the same as being hungry."

"Then I miss Amby," I say sadly.

"Me too," says Electra.

"Families," the captain reminds us. She's right. Amby's family is big and complicated, and I guess they must need Amby more than we do.

That means we're stuck with Fred, and I can't let the baby shapeshifter play any more mean tricks on him.

Suddenly the door slides open and Reetha, who is never in a hurry, hurries back into the mess-room. "Captain," she says.

"Yes?" Captain Astra replies, turning.

"Trouble," Reetha says.

"Yes?" I reply.

"No," Reetha says firmly. *"Trouble."*

Oops. She doesn't mean me; she means something has happened and *trouble* is what we're *in*.

The captain races down the main corridor of
the *Hindsight* to the bridge—the ship's control center—with
me and Electra right behind her.

You'd think a ship's bridge would be all shiny devices and
flashing lights and self-destruct buttons, but the bridge of the
Hindsight is sort of cramped and messy. In its center is the captain's command chair, which is lumpy and has stuffing leaking
out of it. As we arrive, Reetha pushes past us and sits at the
communication station. At the navigation station is Fred, who
twists an eyestalk to glance at us and then goes back to work.
The giant screen at the front of the bridge shows stars stream-
ing past as we zoom along through space.

"What's the problem?" the captain asks, flinging herself
into her command chair. "What are we dealing with here?"

Reetha pushes some buttons, and the screen goes dark and

then shows us a sleek, shiny ship bristling with weaponry. It looks fast and deadly.

"StarLeague," the captain curses.

Electra and I go to stand beside her chair. "I know that ship," Electra says, and she's gone a little pale. "It's the *Arrow*."

"Yeah, I know what it is," the captain says. "Long-range attack ship, heavily armed. It could squish us like a . . . a small, squishy thing."

"It's more of an exploration ship," Electra corrects. "It's famous. It discovered the Pip wormholes and led the colonization of the Maud planetary system way on the edge of the galaxy."

"Whatever," the captain says. "The StarLeague isn't exploring or colonizing anymore, Electra. It's all military all the time. The *Arrow* carries a lot of weapons, and if it's interested in us, we have a problem. Reetha," she snaps. "How close are they?"

"Getting. Closer," Reetha replies.

"It's following the same course we are," Fred says sharply.

"Maybe it picked up the same signal we did," Electra said, "from the *Skeleton*."

"Could be," the captain says, leaning forward and putting her elbows on her knees as she watches the sleek shape of the *Arrow* on the screen. "Hmm. Fred," she orders, straightening. "Plot a change of course. We'll see if it's really us they're after."

"Already done," Fred bites out, and pushes some buttons.

The StarLeague *Arrow* disappears from our screen.

"Well?" the captain says impatiently. "Are they continuing toward the *Skeleton* or coming after us?"

"Just give it a minute," Fred says.

And a moment later the *Arrow* appears on the screen again.

"It's definitely following us," Electra says, sounding worried.

The captain makes a sound like *grrrrr.*

I don't say anything. All I can do is stare at the screen.

You know about the StarLeague. Builds big ships with lots of weapons, makes laws, keeps everything organized, breaks its own laws by stealing children from their parents and training them to be weapons . . .

When she was small, the StarLeague took Electra away from her family and put her into military training. After Electra stopped being a cadet and joined the crew of the *Hindsight*, the captain tried to find Electra's family—she asked The Knowledge, which knows everything—but not even The Knowledge knew where they were. It was like they'd disappeared.

Electra is brave, and fierce, and smart, and stubborn—and even though she would never admit it, there's also a tiny piece of her that is sad. The only thing she remembers about her family is that her mother cried when she was taken away.

I don't like the StarLeague much either. They created me in a military weapons lab. Then I escaped and came to the *Hindsight*. General Smag tried to capture me because the

StarLeague military wanted to use me as a weapon, because I *am* a weapon when I'm in my Hunter shape. When I went to his ship and found Donut and rescued it, I told Smag that if he didn't leave me and Captain Astra and my family alone, I would find his ship, the *Peacemaker*, and I would take it apart, starting with the weapons lab.

As Captain Astra would say, *hah!* Turns out the StarLeague wasn't happy about losing their shapeshifter weapon—me. They banished General Smag, and now he's in charge of a weather station on a remote ice planet on the other side of the galaxy.

And since then, the StarLeague command, still based on the *Peacemaker*, has left us alone. The galaxy's a big place, you know? Maybe they have other things to worry about.

Anyway, it's been three months—a longish piece of time, as humans measure it—since I dealt with the *Peacemaker*, and now the StarLeague is following us again. Why?

The captain nods at Reetha. "Have they attempted to make contact?"

"No," Reetha answers without looking up from her station.

"Rats," the captain curses. "I suppose it's me they want."

Electra frowns. "I'm a former cadet; it's me they want."

I shake my head. "I'm pretty sure it's me they want."

"They want all of us," the captain says.

"They don't want me," Fred complains from the navigation station. Both of his eyestalks swivel toward us. "I'm a good citizen of the StarLeague. I didn't sign up for this. I don't want any trouble!"

"Well, trouble's what you've got," the captain growls.

"Want the Hunter to go over to the *Arrow* and take it apart so they can't follow us?" I offer.

"*No,*" the captain says. "They'll be ready for you this time. It'll get messy."

By *messy* she means somebody—not me—will get hurt, and we don't want that.

"Well then, can we use the stealth-box to hide ourselves?" I ask. The stealth-box is this tricky bit of technology that hides a ship in a little pocket of space.

"Stealth-boxes are against the law!" Fred puts in.

The rest of us ignore him.

"No, we can't use the stealth-box." The captain scrubs her hands through her hair as if she's frustrated.

"Why not?" Electra asks. "It worked before."

"No, it didn't," the captain shoots back. "Remember why?" She points at me. "Because shapeshifters give off a unique energy signal every time they shift, and the StarLeague knows how to track that signal."

I realize what she's talking about. "I wouldn't shift," I say slowly, "but Donut would. It would give us away—it doesn't know any better."

"Exactly." The captain pushes herself up from her chair and heads out.

"Stop!" Reetha orders from the communication station.

The captain freezes, about to take another step toward the door. "What?"

Reetha points at the floor. "Careful. Donut."

The captain follows her pointing finger. And sure enough, one of the tiles that covers the floor is *not* a floor tile at all. As we watch, it quivers and turns into a blob of goo that slides to the side and then starts creeping up a wall. It stops, blending in.

"See?" the captain says. "The shapeshifter energy signal is probably how they found us in the first place. But it's fine. It's totally fine. We're not stopping and we're not changing course. Let them follow us, and if they give us trouble, they can deal with the consequences!"

What she means is me. *I* am the consequences.

I am scared and alone and ravenously hungry.

I am in an icy-cold room made of metal.

Tall people dressed in white, with masks over their faces, are bent over me. They speak to each other, saying sharp-edged words that I can't understand. Blindingly bright lights shine down from overhead. One of the people takes out an instrument, then pokes me with it.

It *hurts*.

It doesn't stop hurting. I try to shift into another shape, to get away, but I can't; something is holding me down.

No, I want to tell them. *Stop*. But I can't talk.

The person with the instrument presses a button, and it hurts even more.

The shape I'm in sees pain as colors—red, with bolts of white and black, and sizzles of silver.

A noise fills my ears, a roaring sound that gets louder and louder until I realize that it's *me* making that sound, and then I'm struggling and panting for breath and waking up in the darkness of my room with the 147 stars stuck to the ceiling and the blankets tangled around me.

The lights flicker on, and a moment later Electra is standing beside the bed, reaching out for my hand.

We share a room. I'm on the top bunk, she's on the bottom.

"You all right, T?" she asks, giving my hand a squeeze. Her tintacles are wrapped in a night-scarf, and she's blinking at the brightness of the light.

I catch my breath and nod— *yes*—because I can't say anything yet. My face is all wet with tears, and I wipe them off with a corner of my blanket.

"Bad dream?" Electra asks, and then she tells the lights to dim.

I nod again.

Letting my hand go, Electra climbs the ladder, then sits on my bunk with her back against the wall. "I thought you were done with those."

"So did I." My voice is shaky. I scooch over and sit next to her, and she puts a comforting arm around my shoulders. I wrap my arms around my legs and rest my chin on my knees, and start to feel better. Electra knows about nightmares. She gets them too, about her time as a cadet, and because of being taken away from her family so young. For a while we took turns having bad dreams and waking each other up. But for both of us it's been a long time. Months.

"I'm all right," I tell her. "It's all right."

"No, T," Electra says seriously. "What the StarLeague did to you is *not* all right."

And yes, that's why I had a bad dream tonight. Because the StarLeague has left us alone for a long time, but now they're after us again. They'd like to arrest the captain and the crew of the *Hindsight*, and they'd like to send Electra back to cadet training.

But the one they really want, the one they're really after—is me.

One time the captain and I talked about what I am, and why the StarLeague will do anything to capture me. We were in the mess-room, and it was the middle of the night.

Well, it's space. It's always the middle of the night.

But the rest of the crew was in their bunks, asleep.

I was eating eggs scrambled with neon cheese powder, Donut was on the counter quietly pretending to be a pile of protein bars, and the captain was slouched on the blue-and-green-patterned, comfortable couch drinking kaff out of a mug with the words GALAXY'S BEST CAPTAIN printed on it. I think it was a present from Reetha.

Captain Astra knew most of the story, but she asked me to

go over it again, to tell about how I was created in a StarLeague lab, and the rest of it. I told her about how they made me as a blob of goo and then injected me with cells from different kinds of people and animals and then forced me to turn into them. They were experimenting.

"Trying to make a weapon," the captain noted. She sounded all relaxed and lazy, but I could see that her hands were clenched tightly around her mug of kaff.

I didn't want her to worry, so I didn't tell her about the nightmares. But that's what I was dreaming about. Being in a lab where military weapons scientists were experimenting on me.

Then I told her how the scientists mashed together a bunch of different kinds of people and animals and ended up creating an extremely terrifying and indestructible weapon-shape, the Hunter. The StarLeague made the Hunter to attack people and ships and probably planets. It is the most dangerous being in the entire galaxy.

"But the Hunter is me too," I told the captain. "I mean, I am the Hunter."

She finished her kaff and leaned down to set the mug on the floor. "And what are you for, Trouble?"

"My job," I told her, "is to protect the people I love and keep them safe."

She blinked and gave me half a smile. "You mean everybody on this ship. Your family."

That's right.

And now my family includes the baby shapeshifter that we rescued from the StarLeague.

In my bunk, I sigh, shaking off the nightmare feeling, and Electra pats me on the shoulder.

"You all right now?" she asks.

"I'm worried about Donut, too," I tell her.

Electra nods, understanding. "You want it to be part of your family, and it's not cooperating."

"Yep," I say.

Donut is bold and tricky and very hard to understand. It has a weird ability to shift *not* into different kinds of people and animals, the way I do, but into *things*. Like the donut and the metallic spiky thing and the pile of protein bars. It doesn't seem to like me very much, or anybody, really, but maybe *like* is the wrong word. When I first shifted into my human form, I had to learn about emotions; I guess it's possible Donut doesn't *have* any emotions. I don't know! I don't know what it remembers about the weapons lab and what it knows or what it wants or what it needs, and if it has bad dreams the way I do, and this makes me feel all kinds of emotions, like *frustration* and *worry* and above all, *sadness*.

The morning after my nightmare, we're still zooming through space toward the *Skeleton*, and the StarLeague *Arrow* is still following at a distance but not shooting at us or anything, and I decide that I'd better go say hello to the rats.

You already know that rats are hyperintelligent and very sneaky beings. After I helped them colonize a StarLeague ship, they decided that I'm a sort of honorary rat, and they like me to visit them once in a while, so after breakfast, I shift into my rat form and sniff out the crack behind a cupboard that the rats use to get into the galley, our kitchen.

I know what you're thinking—*rats* in the *galley*!!???

But they are smart rats and never leave their droppings lying around, and I set out food for them every night so they don't have to gnaw through boxes or make a mess to get something to eat.

Following the rats' scent markers, I scurry through a ventilation tube, along the edge of a corridor, through a grate, and into the cargo bay until I reach the rat-home, their nest. It's a packing crate in a dark corner where Telly never goes. One of the older rats comes to meet me, her whiskers twitching. I let her sniff me, and then she leads me into the crate. It's pretty much a rat paradise in there, full of comfortable bedding and piles of protein bars and lots of friendly-looking rats.

The other rats crowd around me, and then one of them drags out a protein bar, which is good because I'm hungry, as usual, and we have a rat party there in the dark corner of the cargo bay. And I wish that I could teach Donut how to turn into a rat, because unlike me, rats know how to take good care of their babies.

5

When I get back to the mess-room, sneaking into the galley in my rat form, Electra and Captain Astra are in the middle of a loud argument. In the narrow space that is the galley, I shift into my human boy form and, crouching, put on my clothes. Then I crawl to the edge of the counter and peer around it.

The captain has her arms folded and is glaring at Electra. "You have a problem with the way I'm commanding this ship?" the captain bites out.

"I'm saying," Electra shouts, "that I don't like your strategy, and I don't like your tactics."

"Oh *really*," the captain growls. "And I suppose *strategy* and *tactics* are things you know *all* about."

"It was part of my StarLeague training," Electra replies. Her fists are clenched, and her tintacles are an angry white and are lashing wildly around her head.

My stomach growls. I need to eat something. I stand, popping up from behind the counter.

"Gah!" the captain says, flinching away. "Where did you come from?"

I open a cupboard and pull out a couple of protein bars, checking to be sure they're not Donut being difficult. "I went to say hello to the rats."

"There are no rats on my ship," the captain says. She always says this about rats, and she's always wrong.

"Yes there are," I reply. "What's *strategy* and *tactics*?"

"*Strategy*," Electra tells me, while continuing to glare at the captain, "is the big plan during a battle. Captains make strategy. *Tactics* is who gets killed or hurt while carrying out that plan." She points at herself and then at me.

My mouth is full of protein bar, so I can't add anything, like the fact that in my Hunter form I'm pretty much indestructible.

"Are you saying you think I'll put you and Trouble in danger?" the captain asks.

Electra glares at her. "I'm *saying* I don't like your strategy. You know it's a huge risk trying to get to the *Skeleton*. The only reason you're willing to try it is because you have Trouble." Her tintacles have turned an even brighter, burning white—she's furious. "And he's been having terrible—"

"—foot fungus!" I interrupt, because Electra's about to tell the captain about my nightmares coming back, and I don't want her to worry.

They both stare at me. "Foot fungus," the captain says blankly.

I give Electra a Look, and she gives me a tiny nod, understanding. "Yes, it's awful," she says quickly, "and I have to share a room with him. Anyway," she continues, "what are we even *doing* going to the *Skeleton*? It's dangerous, and you haven't explained it, and we want to help but you didn't even ask first and it's not fair."

The captain blinks. "Huh." She scrubs a hand through her curly white hair. "Yeah," she admits. "You're right."

Electra gives a sharp nod. "Of course I am."

"Ordinarily," the captain says, "we wouldn't risk taking the *Hindsight* to the edge of the galaxy to find an abandoned ship that might have been attacked by some mysterious enemy twelve years ago. It could be dangerous."

"*Could* be!?" Electra interrupts.

The captain huffs out a sigh. "It *will* be dangerous, especially with this blasted StarLeague *Arrow* on our tail. My strategy depends on having the Hunter on our side." She nods at me. "I figured you'd be safe enough in that form, Trouble. But I was wrong to assume you'd want to go after the *Skeleton* just because I do." She glances at Electra. "That goes for you too, Electra."

"We get to choose what to do," Electra says firmly.

"Yes," the captain agrees. "Always."

"Good," Electra says, and her tintacles fade to a happier green. "So. Explain the mission. Explain your *strategy*."

"So it's like this." The captain folds her arms. "As you know, there are people who can't live under the military rule of the StarLeague." She looks at us and raises an eyebrow because yes, we are some of those people. "To survive, they need food, medicine, farm equipment, and so on, but the StarLeague tries to choke off their supplies, to starve them out, basically. The *Hindsight* is a cargo ship, and sometimes our cargo doesn't go to StarLeague-approved ports. Sometimes it goes to people who are just trying to survive."

"So we're helping people," I put in.

"Well, yeah," the captain admits. "But we take payment for the supplies. We're not exactly heroes."

"Still," Electra says, "it's a good mission. I choose to go after the *Skeleton*." She gives a brisk nod and goes to sit down on the couch next to a purple pillow that is suspiciously Donut-sized.

Captain Astra turns to me. "What about you, Trouble? What's your choice?"

Hmm. I like that the captain can't decide for me because I'm her kid, or because she's the captain and this is her ship. I get to choose for myself. The part of me that is a kid isn't sure. I have nightmares about the StarLeague, and I know that Electra is being a good friend, trying to protect me and making sure I get to choose.

The pillow on the couch seems to be paying keen attention as I make my decision. Slowly, sneakily, it edges onto Electra's lap. Noticing, she frowns down at it. One of her tintacles gives it a little wave.

Before it can shift into something prickly or sharp, I go over and take it from Electra's lap.

"Well, Trouble?" Captain Astra asks.

"It'll be dangerous," I say, setting the Donut-pillow on the floor.

"Yes," Captain Astra agrees.

"But not more dangerous than I am," I say, because I'm not just a kid, I'm the Hunter, the most powerful person in the galaxy.

The captain laughs. "True."

I take a deep breath, feeling certain about what I want to do. I'm not going to be scared or worried, and I don't have to let the nightmares keep me from helping my captain.

"Asking for trouble?" she says, grinning.

"Yep!" I answer, and the sudden happy feeling inside me makes my human mouth widen into a smile. Hunting for a ghost ship will be an adventure. And we may not be heroes, but I do like the idea of helping people. Maybe I'm like my captain—at heart I'm a little bit of a pirate too. "I choose to do it," I say. "Let's keep going. Let's find the *Skeleton*."

6

We find the *Skeleton*.

It takes us days and days to get there, and the StarLeague *Arrow* follows us the whole way, quietly, sneakily, almost as if it wants us to forget it's there.

When we arrive, the entire crew is crowded into the bridge—the *Hindsight*'s command center. At the communications station, Reetha has put the deep-space scan on the big screen. Fred is at his station, one eyestalk watching the screen, the other on his navigation. The captain is in her chair, and next to her are Telly and Electra and two Shkkka. I squeeze in behind them. They are all taller than I am.

"How long before that StarLeague ship catches up with us?" the captain asks.

"We changed course and now we're hidden by your illegal stealth-box," Fred answers. He really is an excellent navigator. "They won't find us until one of your pet shape-shifters changes shape."

"All right, we'll have to hurry," the captain says. "That's the *Skeleton* over there," she goes on. "See it?"

"No!" I say.

They pay no attention to me. I try jumping to see the screen over Telly's shoulder. Nothing.

"What *are* those things?" Electra asks, because unlike me, she can see the screen.

"Brrrr," Telly says. "Spooky."

I am taller in my Hunter form, but I don't want to scare them all, and I can't shift and give away our position, so I go down on my hands and knees and start crawling through a crowd of legs.

"Yikes!" says Telly, catching a glimpse of me.

"This is easier in my rat form," I mutter to myself, and squeeze between Telly and Reetha.

The captain stands up from her chair. Seeing me, she rolls her eyes. "All right, let Trouble come to the front."

Telly helps me get to my feet, and I edge past him and go to stand next to the command chair. Somehow a fuzzy blue sock has appeared on the floor near the captain's feet.

"You going to put your sock on?" Captain Astra asks.

"It's not a sock," I tell her.

She eyes it dubiously. "Oh. Donut again?"

Yep.

I look up at the screen. It shows space that is endless and velvety black.

"There are no stars," I realize.

"We're too far out," the captain explains. "We're at the edge of the Deep Dark."

The vast, empty space between galaxies is what she means.

"Reetha," she orders. "Put the light on again and get us a close-up of the *Skeleton*."

The screen blurs, there's a flash of light, and the ghost ship appears.

Telly is right. The *Skeleton is* creepy.

You've probably seen lots of ordinary spaceships that are built of metal with a snub nose, big middle with lots of cargo sections, and a stubby tail, no windows, lots of sensor antennae, all beat-up from space dust and random meteor hits.

But this part isn't ordinary: the outer surface of the *Skeleton* is covered with small glowing dots.

"Star-fish," the captain says.

"What are they?" I ask.

"Deep-space creatures," she explains. "Harmless."

On the screen, the star-fish ripple, and one by one they blink out as a crowd of ten-legged creatures appears and scurries after them, clinging to the *Skeleton*'s metal surface with bone-tipped claws.

"Huh," the captain says. "Nebula crabs."

"Are they dangerous?" Electra asks.

"Only to star-fish," Captain Astra says. She leans forward in her seat, elbows on knees, staring at the screen. "Also from deepest space. They shouldn't give us any trouble." She casts a sideways glance at me—because *trouble* is like a secret message between us—and I raise an eyebrow, a human trick that I learned from her.

On the screen, the bony crabs cover the surface of the *Skeleton*. And then another shape appears.

It flows like black smoke under the belly of the ghost ship, a huge snakelike creature. It's so dark, its rippling scales seem to drink in the light. It has a broad snout with deep eyes that swirl like galaxies—and then it opens a gaping maw of a mouth and sucks in one of the crabs. The other crabs scuttle away from it, their bony claws striking sparks off the metal skin of the ship.

"What is *that*?" I ask. I've never seen any creature like it. It is so black that it is *ultra*-black, like a hole in the deep darkness of space.

"Blackdragon," the captain says in a hushed voice, staring at the screen. The blackdragon rests, wrapped around the nose of the *Skeleton*. "Like the star-fish and the crabs, it's a creature of the Deep Dark. Very rare. We don't know much about them."

"Is that what killed the *Skeleton*'s crew?" Electra asks.

The captain gives a little shiver. "We don't know what happened to the *Skeleton*'s crew."

"But it *could* have," Electra says.

"Maybe." She glances at Reetha. "You ever hear of a blackdragon attacking a ship?"

Reetha gives her a blank look. I think it means *no*. Or maybe it means *yes*. You can never be sure, with Reetha.

Then I see something else that makes me gasp and point at the screen.

"What?" the captain asks, turning to me.

"StarLeague," I tell her. Because it's faded and scratched, but there's a StarLeague logo on the outer metal skin of the *Skeleton*.

"Oh. Uh-huh," the captain says after glancing at it.

As if it's no big deal. "The *Skeleton* is a StarLeague ship?"

"Yeah, well, the StarLeague wasn't always the StarLeague."

"What?" I ask, because she's making no sense at all.

"I don't have time for a history lesson right now, kiddo," she says impatiently, and then starts issuing orders to the Shkkka and to Telly, and they leave the bridge. Then she turns to me. "Well, Trouble?" she begins, with another glance at the screen. "What do you think?"

I think I need a history lesson, is what. But instead I say, "The Hunter is going to the *Skeleton*."

"Not by yourself, you're not," Electra says firmly. "Not with that blackdragon out there. I'm coming with you, T."

"That's fine," Captain Astra says. "But get moving. Once you shift, Trouble, the StarLeague *Arrow* will detect us, and I want us to be long gone with the *Skeleton*'s supplies before it gets here."

7

Humans do this weird thing when they're in exciting or dangerous situations. Their own bodies make a fight-or-flight chemical called *adrenaline,* which, I guess, helps them to survive.

Electra and I are at the lockers in the cargo bay, where Electra is climbing into her space suit, which is black and armored and sleek and has the StarLeague logo on one arm. The same logo that is painted on the outside of the *Skeleton.* Electra's logo is left over from when she was a Dart pilot and a cadet.

In case you forgot, when a soft humanoid body goes into the freezing airlessness of deep space without a space suit on, this thing called *ebullism* happens to it. Basically it means the humanoid dies. Gruesomely.

As a shapeshifter who is not actually a human, I do

not have this problem, but still, as Electra gets ready, my currently human body puts some adrenaline into my bloodstream, and it makes me feel twitchy and nervous and jittery. My stomach growls, even though I just ate a giant pile of protein bars.

"Ready?" Electra asks. She reaches into a locker and pulls out a blaster.

"You're not going to need that," I tell her, pointing at the weapon. I don't like guns.

"Just in case," she says, and puts the blaster into a holster on her space suit.

All right, whatever. I shift. As I do, all my human adrenaline and excitement go away, and I become . . . a weapon.

Here's the thing about my Hunter shape.

It is strong. It can walk through walls and move with incredible speed. The Hunter has teeth that drip with poisonous acid, and it is heavily armored, with knife-sharp spikes protruding from its spine, elbows, and shoulders. It can survive unprotected in deepest space. It is the most powerful being in the entire galaxy.

That StarLeague ship that's following us? They'd better *hope* we're gone before they get here, because they do *not* want to deal with the consequences that are the Hunter.

In her sleek space suit, carrying her helmet, Electra clomps over to the airlock. As she pushes the button to open it, the captain comes into the cargo bay, followed by Reetha.

Seeing that I've already shifted into the Hunter, the captain

pauses for half a second—because yes, I am scary-looking—
and then comes over to us.

"Don't bother telling us to be careful," Electra says before
the captain can say anything.

The Hunter can't really talk, but I sort of roar out a laugh,
HAAAAHHHHHAAAAHAAAA!

"Yeesh," the captain says, stepping back, blinking.

I close my mouth. Does the Hunter have bad breath?

"We assume," Electra says, stepping into the airlock, "that
our mission is to check out the *Skeleton* to be sure it's safe, and
to see if its cargo is intact—while avoiding star-fish, nebula
crabs, and the blackdragon."

"That is, in fact, your mission," the captain says dryly.
"And do it fast, because we're on a tight schedule here." Behind
her, Reetha folds her burly arms and stares at us with golden
eyes. I know what she's thinking: *Don't do anything stupid.*

"Come on, T," Electra says, waving me into the airlock.
She ties back her tintacles and then shoves the space suit helmet onto her head and locks it into place.

I step into the airlock with her. It's a cargo airlock, so
there's plenty of room.

"Be careful, you two!" the captain says.

I wave a claw at her and Reetha, and I *know* Electra is rolling her eyes at the advice, but then she hits the button to close
the inner hatch. The door seals, and Electra pushes the button
to open the outer hatch, and we're sucked out of the *Hindsight*
and into deep space. We whirl around and then steady as we

float toward the *Skeleton*, which is lit up by lights from our ship. Electra is propelled by a jet-pack in her space suit; the Hunter just goes where it wants to go.

As we float across the weirdly starless space, all I can do with my sharp Hunter eyes is stare at the blackdragon that is wrapped around the nose of the other ship like a long scarf made of night. It's covering up the StarLeague logo.

When Electra speaks inside her space-suit helmet, my keen Hunter ears can hear her.

"It's weird, isn't it?" she asks, her voice tinny.

It is. It's the strangest, most interesting, most beautiful creature I have ever seen in my entire life.

And then one of its starry eyes catches sight of us.

Slowly, the blackdragon unwraps itself from around the *Skeleton*. Smoothly, silently, it flows away from us. One last glint of its eye, and it melts into the darkness.

Invisible.

But not gone.

8

Electra, who has advanced cadet training,
knows how to get us inside the *Skeleton*. As she's hurrying
to open the outer hatch, I grip a handle with one of my claws
while keeping an eye on the nebula crabs, about ten of them
clinging to the metal skin of the ship about ten feet away from
me. They're not too big; they'd come up to the knees of my
human boy shape. They have beady black eyes and bony bodies with long spidery legs. All of their eyes are fixed on me.

I can't tell if they're afraid of the Hunter—as they should
be—or if they want to try to eat the Hunter—a bad idea.

To test which, I shift toward them, and they all skitter
backward until they're on the other side of the ship, hiding.
Afraid, then. Good.

Hurry up, Electra. She's still fiddling with the outer hatch.

I turn to look out beyond the *Skeleton* into the deepest,

darkest space where there are no stars. Seeing it gives me a creepy feeling, almost like something is out there, watching. Somehow the darkness feels *too* dark, as if it's sucking in all the light.

"*Ugh,*" Electra's tinny voice says. "*T, I can't get this.*" Her space-suited hand points at the *Skeleton*'s hatch. "*Can you . . . ?*"

The Hunter is super fast, as I may have mentioned. It's so fast that I can shift between molecules—basically, I can walk through walls if I need to.

I shift into my speedy mode and step through the curtain of molecules that make up the *Skeleton*'s hatch. To Electra, it looks like I just disappeared. Once inside the airlock, I hit a button to open the outer hatch. Electra floats in.

It's too crowded in the airlock, so once the outer hatch door is closed, I shift into my human shape.

From inside her space-suit helmet, Electra glares at me. "*T, it's not safe,*" her tinny voice says. Then she reaches for the weapon she brought, pulls it out of the holster, and holds it out to me.

I shake my head—*no*.

Then she hits the button that opens the inner hatch, letting us onto the *Skeleton*.

I step through, into a long, empty corridor. There is gravity holding our feet to the floor. It's dark, the only light coming from Electra's helmet, behind me. The air is cold and it smells musty, like it's been cycled through filters for a long time.

Old air—but this ship is not entirely dead.

Hanging on hooks beside the inner hatch is a row of space suits. They look like empty bodies. Creepy.

I hear a hiss of air and turn to see that Electra is taking off her helmet; she sets it on the floor by the airlock. When she straightens, she has the blaster in her hand.

"Look." She points to the row of space suits. "The crew didn't try to escape." Her voice echoes down the dark corridor.

"Or maybe they didn't have time to put them on," I suggest.

"Maybe." She pulls a coverall off another hook and hands it to me.

As you know, when I shift, my clothes don't come with me. Shivering in the cold air, I pull on the coverall, rolling up the legs and the sleeves. It feels weird to be putting on the scratchy old clothes of a crew member who's been gone for so many years. I look down at myself. On the front of the coverall is the StarLeague logo.

Electra is all business. She hits another button on the wall, and blue lights flicker on along the corridor. "We need to move fast," she says. "The cargo area should be down there." With the blaster ready, she leads the way.

"Electra, do you have time for a history lesson?" I ask her as we hurry along the corridor. "Why did Captain Astra say the StarLeague wasn't always the StarLeague?"

She casts me a glance over her shoulder. "The original mission of the StarLeague was to explore the galaxy and help people settle empty planets. I mean, they built ships like the *Skeleton* to run supplies so people could survive out in the remotest parts of the galaxy."

"And now they build ships like the *Peacemaker*," I say.

"Yes," Electra agrees. "Now the StarLeague is like the captain said. All military all the time."

"Why did it change?" I wonder.

"No idea," Electra says. "It happened when I was just a baby. That's when they started building up the military and taking kids away from their families to train them as cadets."

When we reach a door leading off the corridor, I push a button to open it. I poke my nose in. It's the cabin of a crew member, somebody not very neat and tidy—there are clothes strewn across the floor and the bed was left unmade. For the last twelve years. No wonder they call this a ghost ship.

"Leave it," Electra tells me.

As we turn back to the corridor, my ears catch the faintest *skrrtch skrrtch skrrtch* sound. "What was that?" I peer back toward the way we came.

Skrrtch skrrtch.

From out of the shadows at the end of the corridor creeps a cluster of nebula crabs. Their bony legs go *tick-tick-tick* against the floor. It's their mouthparts that are making the *skrrtch* sound.

"Get behind me," Electra snaps, and takes up a firing stance, gripping the blaster with both hands. "Don't come any closer," she shouts at the crabs, "or I will shoot!"

The crabs edge closer. Their mouthparts click. They are *hungry*.

"All right, I warned you," Electra says, and squeezes the trigger of her blaster.

And the weapon loses its shape and melts over her hands. "Gah!" she exclaims as it drops to the floor, where it sits there quivering, a blob of goo.

"Donut!" I say. The baby shapeshifter, up to its tricks again.

And then, *skrrtch skrrtch*, the nebula crabs are on us.

9

With blinding speed, I shift into my Hunter form, and as Electra snatches one crab from her arm, I fling off the rest and they go tumbling down the corridor. They crash into the airlock door, a tangle of bony legs. The Hunter stalks toward them. The crabs freeze in their heap; their beady black eyes are fixed on me.

RAWR, I roar at them, and stomp closer, filling the corridor.

As you know, the Hunter can move incredibly fast when it wants to. The only reason it's rawring and stomping is to give the crabs a chance to escape so it doesn't have to crush them.

Rawr! Stomp! Stomp!

Crawling over each other, the terrified nebula crabs retreat into the airlock; a bony leg hits the button, sealing them in.

I shift back into my human boy shape. "We are *not* for eating!" I call after the crabs.

A moment later, they're off the ship.

The floor is cold under my bare feet as I go back along the corridor to where Electra is waiting for me. "Stupid crabs," she says, inspecting the arm of her space suit to be sure it doesn't have a hole in it.

You know what happens if there's a hole in a space suit, right?

Right. Gruesome death. Not good.

I put on my coverall again.

Electra points at Donut, still a blob of goo on the floor. "What about that?"

I crouch and pick Donut up. "Can you shift into a scarf, or something," I ask it, "so I don't have to carry you?"

In my hands, the blob of goo shimmers. It's warm and heavier than it looks. And it doesn't shift.

"All right," I say, and put it inside the coverall, and then fasten it up the front. Having Donut in there makes it look like I have a fat belly.

Even though what I really have is a very empty belly. All of this shifting is making me ravenously hungry.

"Come on," Electra says sharply. "Captain Astra and the rest will be getting impatient."

"*Getting?*" I ask.

"Ha ha," Electra answers, because we both know that Captain Astra is not the most patient person in the galaxy. Especially when she's got the StarLeague *Arrow* on the way.

We hurry along the corridor until we get to an armored

door leading to the cargo bay. Electra opens it and we go in.

The *Skeleton*'s cargo area is a cavernous space filled with sealed boxes and bins and cargo pods, all with the StarLeague logo on them. It's *cold*. Our breath comes out as ice crystals that freeze in the air and drop to the floor. My human boy shape starts to shiver. I would shift into the Hunter, except I want to keep baby Donut with me, so I wrap my arms around myself and follow Electra as she clomps across the floor to the nearest cargo pod.

With her gloved hand she wipes frost off a panel, leaning close to read it. "Telly was right," she says. "The cargo is in stasis." She pats the side of the pod. "This one contains vegetable seeds. Just think how many people those seeds will feed." She goes to another pod and checks the panel. "Hah. This one is full of protein bars. More than even *you* could eat, T."

As an answer, my stomach growls so loudly that it almost echoes in the cavernous space.

Electra glances at me, then looks again, frowning. "Trouble, you're turning *blue*."

"I'm all r-r-r-ight," I say. I think my face is going to freeze off.

"There are ice crystals on your eyelashes," Electra points out. "Shift into the Hunter before you turn into an ice cube."

"C-c-can't," I say, and pat the bump that is Donut.

Electra nods, understanding. Then she grabs my arm and drags me out of the cargo bay, sealing the door behind us. The corridor isn't much warmer.

"Come on," she says. "We need to report to Captain Astra." Taking my hand, she pulls me toward the airlock. She puts on her helmet, and I hand her Donut and then shift into the Hunter. A moment later we're out the *Skeleton*'s airlock, floating in space.

And . . .

The *Hindsight* has disappeared.

10

There's nothing around us but the starless dark.

And that weird, creepy feeling again, like we're being watched. Even though we're completely alone.

Electra and the Hunter float away from the *Skeleton*, and we're both staring at the empty space where our ship is supposed to be.

Electra is checking a panel on the sleeve of her space suit. *"It's gone,"* she says. *"I'm not getting any readout at all."*

Then my keen Hunter eyes catch a glimmer of light. Looking closer, I see what has happened.

The *Hindsight* is here, but it's completely wrapped in the night-black coils of the blackdragon.

Here's how my shapeshifting works.

If I get near enough to another living thing, I can shift into that form. Maybe a bit of DNA or a cell of the other creature or person is floating around and I take it in, and the shifter part of me makes sense of it, and I don't even have to think about it, I just know that I can shift. I am still me, but shaped like the other creature, down to my bones—if it has bones— down to my cells, down to my DNA.

Electra floats next to me in the darkness. I can see that inside her space-suit helmet she's frowning. If she's getting no readout on the *Hindsight*, she might really think it's gone.

Then the blackdragon moves, its soft black coils loosening, and part of our ship is revealed—an outer hatch leading to an airlock.

Catching Electra's eye, I point at myself with a claw, then at the blackdragon.

"*All right,*" she says. "*I'm not telling you to be careful, T, but . . .*"

I know, I know. So while she and Donut jet over to the *Hindsight*'s airlock, I head for the blackdragon that is curled around our ship.

The Hunter shape is very terrifying, so even though I can imagine Captain Astra's voice telling me to *hurry because the StarLeague is coming*, I go slowly, drifting under the *Hindsight*'s middle.

I get closer.

From this close, the blackdragon doesn't look scaly, but

weirdly fluffy, like a scarf knitted out of darkness. But it's huge.

It's big enough to open its mouth and eat the Hunter whole.

Of course, if that happened, the Hunter would fight its way out of the blackdragon's belly, so that wouldn't end well for it.

The blackdragon's starry eyes watch as the Hunter drifts closer . . .

. . . and closer. Its black scales are like velvet, and so deep and dark that they seem to suck in the light. So beautiful.

I want to see it.

I want to *be* it.

When I'm done talking to the blackdragon and it's loosened its grip on our ship, I get back to the *Hindsight*. Reetha opens the airlock for me, points at a pile of clothes she's dropped on the floor, and without saying anything heads off in the direction of the cargo bay.

As I'm putting the clothes on, the captain and one of the Shkkka hurry down the corridor toward me. They pass and the captain snaps, "Get something to eat, Trouble, and then come help in the cargo bay. We're linking up with the *Skeleton* and we have to get the supplies on board and get out of here *fast*." She turns and jogs backward so she can yell one more thing at me. "And *what* is going on with that blackdragon?! How did you get it to let us go?"

I don't have time to answer before she's turned and raced off.

On my way to the galley, I pass another Shkkka, who waves at me with her antennae and hurries past.

In the galley I chomp a protein bar while mixing up noodles and neon cheese powder, and I'm so hungry from shifting that my stomach is practically roaring.

I'm also feeling a little weird, sort of empty and stretched out and lonely. Blackdragons are not like anything else I've ever shifted into before. I'm also prickly because of that being-watched feeling I had out there in space. It's just the ghost ship and the Deep Dark, I tell myself. They're creepy.

I'm slurping up my second bowl of noodles when the captain, Fred, and Reetha hurry through on their way to the bridge, the captain snapping out orders about *getting underway* and *evasive maneuvers*.

I'm busy making a third delicious cheesy huge bowl of noodles when Electra comes in and flops on the couch. Her tintacles are green and limp. "Phew!" she sighs.

"Did you get all the treasure off the *Skeleton*?" I say through a mouth full of noodles.

"Yes, we did," she says wearily.

A moment later the captain comes in, rubbing her hands together. "We're away," she tells us. "No sign of the StarLeague. And Telly has already lined up some people who can use the supplies. We are *set*." She goes into the galley and starts making a cup of kaff. "Trouble," she calls, "you need to keep Donut from shifting, if you possibly can, so the StarLeague can't use the shifter energy to track us now that we've set a new course."

"I'll try," I say, looking around the mess-room. It's full of things, like pillows and socks and dishes—and any of them could be Donut, hiding.

The captain pokes her head out of the galley. "And you don't shift either, Trouble," she reminds me. "Unless you absolutely have to."

"I know," I say, and take another bite of noodles.

She comes out and takes a big drink of kaff. "Ahhhh. So, kiddo. How did you deal with the blackdragon?"

Oop. She's not going to like this.

11

"**Well, Trouble?**" **the captain says.** "**The black-**
dragon? How did you get it to let us go?"

I do a very human-like thing: I smile. Not a happy smile,
more an apologetic one. "Well, I . . . um . . . I shifted."

She sets her mug down on the table with a thump. Kaff
sloshes out. "You *shifted* into a *blackdragon*?"

"Yep," I admit.

"Gah," the captain says, and flings herself into her chair
at the head of the table. Then she jumps to her feet again and
paces to the other end of the mess-room and back. "Trouble, I
know you're powerful in the Hunter form, but getting that close
to a blackdragon was too big a risk." She turns to Electra, who
is still flopped out on the couch. "Why didn't you stop him?"

"Oh, sure," Electra says, with an eyeroll. "When was the
last time *you* stopped Trouble from doing something he was
determined to do?"

The captain glares.

"That's what I thought," Electra says smugly. "Never."

"All right," the captain mutters. "Fine." She collapses into her chair. "While you two were taking forever checking out the *Skeleton*, we all got a little nervous when the blackdragon wrapped itself around the ship, so I sent a message to The Knowledge, asking for information."

In case you don't know, The Knowledge is a strange and interesting thing . . . being . . . creature . . . person.

I'm not sure what it is, actually.

Like me, The Knowledge was created in a StarLeague lab. It was made to know everything. Anything it doesn't know, it desperately wants to learn about. It lives . . . inhabits . . . exists . . . whatever . . . in an asteroid that is covered with antennae and other devices so that all of the information in the entire galaxy flows to it.

"Here's what The Knowledge told me." The captain takes a sip of kaff and makes a face at its bitter taste. I don't know why she keeps drinking it, since it's so awful. "Blackdragons," she tells us, "are creatures of deepest space."

I nod. This is true.

"There shouldn't be a blackdragon within a quintillion miles of the galaxy's edge," the captain goes on.

Also true.

A quintillion is a real number, by the way. It's a one followed by eighteen zeros. 1,000,000,000,000,000,000. A quintillion miles is a *long* way. It means blackdragons belong in space so deep, so dark, that not even starlight goes there.

"So why is it here?" Electra asks. "Where it's not supposed to be?"

"I asked that question," the captain says. "The Knowledge said it didn't know the answer."

I blink. "But The Knowledge knows everything."

The captain shrugs. "Not this time. And yeah, I know. It's weird."

"Did the blackdragon tell you anything, T?" Electra asks, sitting up. Her tintacles are an alert, interested green.

They both turn and look at me.

I twirl a bite of noodles around my fork. "*Tell* isn't exactly the right word," I say. I'm not sure I can explain to them what it's like being a blackdragon. Slowly, I set down my fork and then climb into the nest chair. Human legs only bend one way, so I cross them in front of me and settle in. It's a comfortable, comforting way to sit, and it makes me miss Amby, who always sits like this. "This blackdragon is young," I tell them, "and small. For its kind."

"So it's like . . . a child?" the captain asks.

"Yep," I say. "A kid like us." I point to myself and to Electra. Then I tell them how blackdragons live in the deepest space between galaxies. They live for thousands of years and never stop growing—a blackdragon can grow big enough to stretch across an entire solar system. Their thoughts are vast and slow, and usually they don't do much but drift out there. And all the time they sing—they sing deep, endless songs to other blackdragons across the starless dark.

In my blackdragon form I could *feel* the other blackdragon's song vibrating through me.

In all of the vastness of space, nobody was singing back.

The blackdragon wrapped around our ship—it is young, and sad, and lonely, and . . . something else.

"It's afraid," I tell Captain Astra and Electra.

"Afraid," the captain repeats. "Of what?"

"I don't know," I say. "But the star-fish, and the nebula crabs, and the blackdragon—I think they're all here inside our galaxy, where they're not supposed to be, because they're hiding. They're afraid of something in the Deep Dark."

And then I tell the captain that I promised the kid blackdragon that it could come with us.

"You did *what*!?" she yells at me, while Electra laughs. "The blackdragon can*not* come with us!"

"But it's lost!" I tell her.

"It's not like picking up a . . . a *puppy*," the captain says.

"To Trouble it is," Electra puts in.

"It might be the very last blackdragon in the entire universe," I say. "It's alone." I know about being alone. I used to think I was the only one of my kind, until we found the baby shapeshifter.

The captain knows this. She sighs. "All right, Trouble. Fine. The blackdragon can come with us."

"It doesn't really need our permission," I say. "I mean, nobody says *no* to a blackdragon."

12

Captain Astra and her crew—including me and Electra—are not pirates, exactly, but we do operate outside the laws of the StarLeague. We keep a low profile and go about our business, and we don't hurt anybody, and up until now the StarLeague has pretended we don't exist, and that way everybody's been happy and the Hunter didn't have to go take apart a StarLeague ship.

Then there are those people who Electra told me about. The ones who live outside the StarLeague's law. Some of them are rebels, and some are criminals, and some practice weird religions, and some have strange eating habits, and some are farmers who just want to be left alone. Some of them are dangerous, and the rest of them are . . . also dangerous.

Anyway, these people need supplies: medicine, food, seeds, machinery, fuel, things like that. A ship's crew that can deliver these things—secretly, without the StarLeague knowing—can help those people, and also they can make a lot of money.

I don't really understand money, or care about it, but Captain Astra does. She told me that she doesn't entirely own the *Hindsight*. She says that it costs so much money to buy a ship that she's been paying for it over many years, and she has people pressuring her because she still owes them more money. *You know how you're hungry all the time, Trouble?* she asked me. *These people are hungry too, but not for food. They want money, and when you give them some, they just want more. I don't have any choice. I have to pay them regularly or they will take the ship.*

With the baby blackdragon wrapped around the middle of our ship, we are heading for an abandoned space station where we will meet up with people who will pay a lot of money for the *Skeleton*'s supplies. The station is a secret—it's not on any of the official starmaps in our galaxy. Captain Astra knows where it is, and Fred is a good enough navigator to get us there. The name of the space station is Dread-knot, and it should take us three days to reach it.

But it ends up taking us more time than that.

That's because we were halfway to Dread-knot when the captain came into the galley to make some kaff. I was there making a delicious stew dinner for the crew when she pushed past me, grabbed her mug out of a cupboard, and set it on the counter.

The mug had **GALiXYS beST CaTPiAN** written on it.

I was puzzling out the words—why was it spelled wrong?—when the captain tried to pour hot kaff into it.

You probably figured it out before I did. The mug was Donut. You can imagine what a mess that was, plus there was shouting, and then Donut turned into a dust ball and went and hid under Electra's bed.

But because it shifted, it gave off that special shapeshifter energy, which meant the StarLeague picked us up again, and despite some tricky navigational maneuvers by Fred, the *Arrow* is still following us.

That's a problem. We can't lead the StarLeague to Dreadknot Station. They would arrest the people we're going to sell the *Skeleton*'s supplies to. So the captain has stopped the ship and we're just sitting here in space with a kid blackdragon curled around our ship. Waiting.

And the StarLeague *Arrow* is sitting in space not far away. Crowding us just a little. Making sure we know it's watching us. And waiting.

"I don't get it," Captain Astra says at dinner, when everybody's twitchy with nervousness and hardly eats anything. "That *Arrow* could squish us like a . . ."

". . . bug?" I ask.

"Like a grape?" Telly puts in, looking up from his vegetarian dinner.

"Like a squishy thing?" Electra says, with an eyeroll.

"You people," the captain says, pushing her plate away and putting her elbows on the table. "I'm serious. This StarLeague ship is behaving very strangely." She counts off on her fingers. "One, they're just sitting there. Two, they haven't sent a Dart ship to bother us. Three, they haven't fired a weapon at us. Four . . ." She breaks off. "Reetha, have they attempted to contact us?"

"No," Reetha grunts.

"Four, no attempt at contact. So what do they *want*?"

One of Electra's tintacles points at me.

"I agree," the captain says. "They want Trouble. Why don't they try to take him?"

I'm busy eating everybody's leftovers. "The Hunter," I say.

"They want the Hunter but they don't want to deal with the Hunter?" The captain pushes herself to her feet. "It doesn't make sense, and not even the StarLeague is this stupid. There's something going on, and I don't like it." She pauses in the doorway. "Until we figure it out, we're not going anywhere."

So. It's a standoff.

13

It's very late at night, and Electra is asleep in the lower bunk. Earlier she pulled dust-ball Donut from under her bed and asked it to shift into its purple pillow form, and surprisingly it did, adding bright yellow stripes, and now it's snuggled up next to her.

But I can't sleep. The StarLeague ship is out there. Usually waiting patiently and watching is not the way the StarLeague does things. The captain is right—the *Arrow* is acting strangely.

And I'm going to do something about it. But first I have to eat. A lot.

Quietly, I push back the covers, climb down the ladder, and go out of our room and along the corridor to the mess-room.

The lights are dim, and the captain is there, lying on the blue-and-green patterned couch with her eyes closed.

But she's not asleep; I can tell.

Maybe she's listening to the singing of the stars, which is something she does when she's alone in the dark.

Leaving the lights dim, I go to the kitchen, where I make a cup of kaff for her and four bowls of stew for me. As I carry it out of the galley on a tray, she sits up.

"Hey, kiddo," she says wearily, and takes the mug. "Thanks."

I sit on the floor with my back against the couch and take a bite of stew. Mmmm. Cubes of vegetable, cubes of protein, all in a salty brown sauce. Stew is about my favorite thing in the entire galaxy.

While I eat, the captain stretches out on the couch again, holding the mug of kaff on her stomach, staring at the ceiling. When I'm done, I pile the stew bowls on the floor and we're both quiet for a while. I really need to get going—because I've come up with a plan for dealing with the StarLeague ship— but the captain's hand is resting on the top of my head. It makes me feel safe.

Suddenly my stomach gives a loud, hungry growl.

The captain snorts. "I heard that."

"Heard what?" I say, pretending I have no idea what she's talking about.

"I swear, kid," she says. "You just demolished four huge bowls of stew. I've never seen anybody eat as much as you do."

"It's because I'm always hungry," I tell her.

"Your stomach is a black hole," she jokes.

But I don't laugh. Because I've just realized how we can hide from the StarLeague ship. "The blackdragon!" I exclaim.

"Huh?" The captain sits up, blinking, as I get to my feet.

"When Electra and I went over to the *Skeleton*," I tell her. "We were on our way back and we thought the *Hindsight* was gone because it was wrapped up in the blackdragon. Electra wasn't getting any readings at all."

"Our ship was completely hidden?" she asks.

"Undetectable," I say. "The Hunter couldn't see it either," I tell her, "and it can detect things even better than a ship's sensors."

"Uh-oh," she says slowly. "I see what you're getting at. You think the blackdragon can hide us from the StarLeague *Arrow* so we can continue to Dread-knot Station?"

"Yep!" I say. "We can just sneak away."

The captain raises an eyebrow. "You can just ask it?"

"Sing to it," I correct. "But yes." I give her a happy grin. "I wish you could come with me. You'd love seeing the black-dragon up close."

"No, I wouldn't!" she says, and then shakes her head. "All right. I'm not going to stop you. Go do it."

I head for one of the *Hindsight*'s outer hatches. Yes, I'm going to ask the blackdragon to hide us. But first, I have something else to do.

Look out, StarLeague *Arrow*. The Hunter is coming.

14

Thinking about what I'm about to do makes
my human heart beat very quickly—because of adrenaline!—but
when I get to the airlock, I shift into my Hunter form and feel a lot
more fierce. And also hungry, but I'll eat again when I get back.
Before opening the outer hatch, I remember to grab my Trouble
clothes in a claw because I'm going to need them. Then I hit the
button, the airlock opens, and the Hunter is sucked outside.

As always, space is icy cold and airless. I head toward the
StarLeague *Arrow*, which is a sleek silver shape like a shark
floating in the distance. Behind me, the *Hindsight* is a scuffed
tin can of a ship with a soft black scarf—the blackdragon—
wrapped around one end.

As you know, the Hunter could easily break into the *Arrow*
and stomp and rawr and take it apart.

But I'm not going to do that.

Think about it. The *Arrow* knows what the Hunter is capable of; they know how dangerous I am. And yet they've been following the *Hindsight* all over the galaxy without firing so much as a shot. They don't want a fight. They want something else, and I'm going to find out what it is.

The Hunter gets closer to the *Arrow*. I figure I'll have to shift through an outer wall to get in, but then I spy an outer hatch—and it's open. They must have detected the energy signal when I shifted into my Hunter form, and now their sensors have picked me up. They know that I'm coming.

The Hunter floats into the airlock; the outer hatch door closes with a *whoosh* and the inner door opens. Ready for a fight, the Hunter leans out, peering down a brightly lit corridor. It's empty in both directions, but a row of lights along the floor blinks, leading away. Stepping out, the Hunter lopes along, following the lights. They lead left, then right, along silent corridors until they reach a door, where they blink out.

It could be a trap.

But somehow I doubt it. With a claw I reach out and tap on the door. *Hello! Let me in!*

The door whisks open. The Hunter steps onto the bridge of the StarLeague ship.

The *Arrow*'s command center is way fancier than the one on my own ship. The floor is gleaming metal, and there are ranks of stations for navigation, communication, weapons, sensors, all of that, busy with blinking lights and readouts. Nobody's sitting at the stations, though. The bridge is nearly empty.

This is good. StarLeague soldiers usually have blasters and a bad habit of firing them at me. It's safer without them.

Safer for *them*, I mean.

There's only one person in the room, sitting in a command chair on a raised platform.

From over by the door, the Hunter examines her.

And she examines the Hunter.

The officer is humanoid; she has wrinkly brown skin and a wide face with a small bump for a nose. Instead of hair, she has what looks like a hard shell covering her head, with horn-like whorls where a human's ears would be. Her eyes are dark brown and are protected by a heavy brow ridge.

"Greetings," she says. Her voice is calm, and she speaks slowly. "I am StarLeague Commander Io. I expected you to enter my ship before this, shapeshifter. I want to speak with you."

Here's the thing. I don't have to talk to her at all. I could just go mess up their ship engine so they can't follow us until they get it fixed. But she's been awfully persistent, and oddly patient, and she doesn't seem to be afraid of me, and I'm curious.

The Hunter drops the clothes it's been carrying onto the floor, and I shift into my human boy shape; quickly, I get dressed and turn to face the StarLeague officer. "I wish the clothes came with me," I say. "But they don't."

"Please come here," Commander Io says.

A polite StarLeague officer? Weird. Still, I cross the gleaming metal floor of the bridge until I'm standing in front of her command chair.

Commander Io's deep brown eyes study me for a few moments. "Ah," she says. "I see. You are very young, aren't you."

"I'm a kid," I tell her.

She nods. "That would make a certain sense."

I look carefully at her. Her wrinkly face seems . . . *kind*. As if she's a nice person. But she can't be. Can she? And she seems strangely familiar. "Have I met you before?" I say slowly.

"*Have* you?" she asks.

"I don't know," I admit. I don't think she's one of the people from my nightmares. She doesn't *seem* to be.

"What do they call you?" she asks.

"My name," I tell her, "is Trouble."

"Mm. I understand there is another like you on the *Hindsight*?"

I shrug because I'm not going to tell her anything at all about the baby shapeshifter. I decide it's time for me to get to the reason why I'm here. "Why are you following us?"

Commander Io is silent for a long moment. Then she says, "You and the other shapeshifter exist for a purpose. Do you know what that purpose is?"

"You're not exactly answering my question," I say.

"Do you know what that purpose is?" she repeats.

All right. Fine. "To be a weapon," I answer.

She cocks her sleek-shelled head. "That is true, Trouble, but not completely true, and not in the way you think. I will answer your question about why this ship has been tracking you and the other shapeshifter. We cannot force you to come with us, but you must allow yourselves to be taken aboard this ship."

"What?" I say, and take a step back. "No."

"You must," she repeats. "It is nearly time for you to fulfill your actual purpose. For you are more than just a weapon."

"I already know *that*," I tell her.

Commander Io gets to her feet and steps down from the command chair. Strangely, she stretches out her hand toward me, but I step back again, out of her reach. "The fate of the entire galaxy may be at stake," she says quietly.

"The *galaxy*?" I repeat. I can imagine the eyeroll from Electra if she heard that one.

"You don't believe me," Commander Io observes, lowering her hand. "That is not surprising. So you will return to the *Hindsight*?"

"Yep," I say.

"We will continue to follow you," she says.

Oh no, you won't, I think, because the Hunter is planning to stop off in her ship's engine room to do some damage.

"In the meantime, Trouble, take with you a message for your captain. It is this." Commander Io climbs back into her command chair. Her voice is steady and she still seems weirdly calm. Her words, though, hit me like a blaster bolt.

"Tell Captain Astra that she and her ship are in very great danger. Far greater than she knows. She has two shapeshifters aboard. She should think of them as bombs." She pauses, her brown eyes steady. "And it is almost time for them to explode."

15

Just so you know, I'm not a bomb that's about to explode.

I'm *not*.

And neither is Donut. At least, I don't *think* it is.

I really have no idea what Commander Io is talking about.

I don't want her following us, so after the Hunter leaves the StarLeague *Arrow*, I circle the ship until I find a weapon—a laser cannon for shooting at other spaceships. Shifting into my blob of goo form, I ooze into the cannon, and from there, deeper into the *Arrow*'s engine. It's a dark, cramped, noisy space lit by flashing blue lights. Bolts of plasma crackle and spark. My goo extends a pseudopod and breaks off a key engine component. I'm not sure what to do with it—and I'm ravenous from all the shapeshifting I've been doing—so . . . I eat it. Yep, I just take it into my goo self, and strangely, it makes me feel less hungry. I break off a few more delicious engine parts, and as alarms blare and the engine makes unhappy noises, I ooze back outside the ship, where I shift into my Hunter form.

Goodbye, StarLeague *Arrow*! Hope we never see you again!

I also stop off to shift into my blackdragon shape, and sing to the other blackdragon. By the time I get back inside the *Hindsight*, it is wrapped around us so we are hidden. Not just black as space, but hidden from the StarLeague *Arrow*'s sensors, so it won't know which direction we're going when we leave.

"What took you so long?" Captain Astra asks, once I'm reporting to her on the cramped, shabby bridge of the *Hindsight*.

"Well . . ." I take a protein bar out of my pocket and start unwrapping it. "I went over to the *Arrow* and talked to its commander."

"Trouble!" The captain makes a gesture with her hands like she wants to strangle something. At the communication station Reetha shakes her head, and from navigation Fred flicks an eyestalk glance at me.

"I was careful," I protest. "And I disabled their engine. Not enough to put anybody on the ship in danger, but enough that it'll take them some time to fix." And then I tell her all about Commander Io—what she looks like and how she's polite and how nobody over there attacked me.

"She had a shell over her head?" Captain Astra asks. "Wrinkly skin?"

"Yep," I say. I put a big bite of protein bar into the black hole that is my stomach. I guess the engine parts are in there too, but they're not bothering me.

"Cycad," Reetha puts in, turning to face us.

"A problem," Captain Astra says with a nod.

I don't get it. "Why is Commander Io a problem?" I ask. "I actually kind of liked her."

"You like everybody," the captain says with an eyeroll.

"No, I don't," I protest. "I don't like General Smag."

"Yeah, well, he was incompetent," Captain Astra says. "This time the StarLeague was smart, sending a Cycad after us. The Cycad species is extremely long lived. Commander Io is probably thousands of years old, maybe more, and that makes her very, very patient. And clever, and even more persistent than General Smag was. She's not going to stop following us anytime soon, even if you did disable her ship." She leans back in the command chair and frowns. "Anything else?" she asks me. "Commander Io never tried to contact our ship, so she must have wanted to talk to you, and only you. What did you talk about with her?"

Um. "Do Cycads tell the truth, usually?"

"They're known for it," Captain Astra answers. "They're a highly moral species. Why? What did Commander Io say to you?"

"Nothing," I say, and the lie tastes funny in my mouth. "I just went in and warned her to quit following us and then disabled the ship. That's all. Nothing else. We didn't talk much. Or at all, really."

"*Really,*" Captain Astra drawls.

"Really," I say firmly.

Apparently, shapeshifters aren't nearly as truthful as Commander Io's species is. Because I don't say anything to Captain Astra about *danger* and *shapeshifters* and *bombs about to explode*. Nope. Not a thing.

After three days of travel past a couple of star systems and out into an empty region of the galaxy—with no StarLeague *Arrow* in sight—we arrive at Dread-knot Station to meet the people who want to buy the supplies we scavenged from the *Skeleton*.

I spend most of the three days being a good galley boy, and trying to keep track of Donut, and making sure the black-dragon is still with us, and also feeling terrible. I *lied*. To *my captain!*

I don't tell Electra about what Commander Io said, either. It feels strange and wrong to keep a secret from my best friend and from my captain, but I don't want them to worry about me or Donut exploding, even though we're *not* bombs.

Yes, I know, I lied to them before, when I first came onto the *Hindsight* and pretended to be an actual human boy and not a shapeshifter who escaped from a level-four military weapons lab. But it's different now. Maybe because back then neither of them trusted me, but now they *do*.

Dread-knot used to be a bright, busy space station where people lived and ships would stop off to be refueled and pick up cargo. But hundreds of years ago it was hit by a piece of space junk and half destroyed. Now it's been abandoned for a long time, floating in the darkness with no ships coming and going.

Except for the people who live outside the rule of the StarLeague. They use the Dread-knot as a secret place to do their deals and pick up the supplies they need to survive.

And the *Hindsight* uses it too, sneaking in, hidden in the folds of the blackdragon.

"This could be dangerous," Captain Astra says as we're about to dock, linking our ship to the Dread-knot. She glances at Telly, who nods, showing that he's ready.

The captain and Telly, along with me and Electra, are in the corridor where our airlock will link up with the station's outer hatch so we can walk on board.

"Trouble, you and Electra don't have to come," the captain adds. She and Telly are not wearing any obvious weapons, but they each probably have a blaster or a laser knife on them somewhere, and Telly has a tablet with a list of the *Skeleton*'s supplies that we'll try to sell here. "We can deal with this ourselves, if we have to. Your choice."

"Don't be silly," Electra says. Her tintacles are tied back and she's wearing a blaster in a holster—she knows it's not

Donut making trouble, because it's still in its stripy pillow form. For now.

"We're coming with you," I tell the captain. I'm wearing my usual coverall and brightly colored sweater, and my feet are bare. There are four protein bars in each of my pockets.

"All right," Captain Astra says with a brisk nod. "I have not dealt with these people before. They are outlaws, and even though we're trying to help them, they may resort to piracy. Once they've had a look at us, they may think they can take our cargo without paying for it." She catches my eye. "Fortunately, we have ways of discouraging that kind of behavior."

Me. I'm the way.

"Let's go," Captain Astra says.

When I was on a space station before, it was all clean metal and bright lights and people rushing around doing important things.

Dread-knot is nothing like that. Once the *Hindsight* has linked up with it, we emerge from our ship's airlock, stepping through a hatch and into a narrow corridor that is dimly lit by lights that flicker, as if the power supply isn't very good. The floor is dirty and there's all kinds of junk scattered around— old screws and bits of wire and food wrappers—and the walls are made of bare, rusty metal. The air smells stuffy and moldy, like the filters aren't working right.

"Nice," Electra comments, looking around.

"Which way?" Captain Astra asks.

Telly shrugs. "This place is a maze. The outlaws said they'd send somebody to meet us."

"Well, they'd better hurry up," the captain grumbles.

A moment later, a huge shape looms up in the dark corridor, lumbering toward us. Captain Astra straightens and puts a hand on her blaster.

As the shape gets closer, I see that it's a hairless, pink-skinned, pink-eyed humanoid with weapons strapped across his chest and a blaster holstered on each hip. He is so broad and tall that he almost blocks the entire hallway. He has a tattoo of a flower that swirls around one eye and extends tendrils over his bald head. His eyes narrow as he studies us. "What's your business?"

Captain Astra gives him a lazy smile. "My business is with whoever does business on this heap of junk." She cocks an eyebrow. "Is that you?"

"No, it ain't," the big man says. Then he jerks a chin toward the hatch leading to our ship. "We watched you come in. What's that *thing* wrapped around the end of your ship?"

"Oh, the blackdragon?" the captain answers with a shrug. "Think of it as a kind of pet."

"A *pet*?" the man asks dubiously. "And this one?" He points at Telly, who bares his tusks.

"Our cargo specialist," the captain tells him.

The big man sneers and points at me and Electra. "An' I

suppose these two kids are your cargo handlers?"

"No," the captain says calmly. "They're my bodyguards."

"Riiiiight," the big man says. He rubs his nose, deciding. "You want to deal, you got to talk to Min."

"Lead on," Captain Astra says.

As we follow the big man down the cluttered corridor, the captain whispers over her shoulder, "Stay alert. These are not friendly people."

"Yeah," Electra whispers back. "We got that."

The captain turns back, marching along beside Telly.

"Should I shift into the Hunter?" I whisper to Electra.

She shakes her head. "Not yet. Hopefully not at all, because the *Arrow* is out there somewhere, and they'll use your shifting as a way to track us. But be ready."

The big man leads us down the corridor, around a corner, and through a bigger empty space. Our footsteps echo on the metal floor.

"Doesn't anybody live here?" I whisper to Electra.

"No," she whispers back. "The captain told me the outlaws live on a secret moon somewhere. They only do their deals here."

We arrive at a rusty armored door. The big man raises a hand, stopping us. "You want to talk to Min, your weapons stay out here."

For a second I think he means me.

Then Captain Astra pulls a small blaster from an inner pocket of her jacket, Telly reaches down and unstraps a knife from his lower leg, and Electra unholsters her blaster. They hand the weapons over.

"What about you?" the big man says to me. "You got any weapons on you?"

"I *am* a weapon," I tell him.

He looks me up and down and snorts. "Sure you are, kid."

"Don't say I didn't warn you," I say.

"*Trouble,*" Electra chides, and gives me a wide-eyed stare that means *Don't be stupid.*

The big man ignores us, going to the rusty metal door and pulling a lever to open it. The door slowly creaks open, revealing a high-ceilinged, echoing room that is full of shadows except in its center, where a beam of light shines down, making a circle on the floor. A dark figure stands at the edge of the light.

"That's Min," the big man tells us. "You want to deal, you talk to her." Then he makes a huge fist and holds it up threateningly. "And be polite. Or else."

16

We cross the darkened room toward Min, whoever she is.

"Greetings," an icy voice says. The figure steps out of the shadows and into the circle of light.

Just like Electra, the woman named Min has hair tintacles, but hers are longer, and they're unbound, writhing around her head like a bunch of blue eels. Her skin is pale green. She's wearing a plain, patched coverall with the sleeves ripped off, and she's tall, standing with muscly arms folded, looking cool and strong and in control.

I try to remember. Electra's tintacles were blue when I first met her. Her tintacles show her emotion, and I think blue is for . . .

"You're Tintaclodian," Electra blurts out, staring at the woman.

"So are you," the woman notes, seeming uninterested, because Tintaclodians are a pretty common galactic species, and turns to address the captain. "Who are you?"

"I'm Captain Astra of the *Hindsight*," my captain answers, "operating outside the StarLeague's control." She points at Telly. "This is my cargo master. He's been in touch with you. As you know, we have supplies, if you've got money. Are you willing to deal with us?"

Min gives a slow nod. "What have you got?" Her blue tintacles are waving around her head, almost like they're trying to get her attention. She raises a hand to smooth them down.

"Seeds," Captain Astra says. "Other foodstuffs, some farm equipment, medical supplies. Pay us market rate, and they're yours."

"A very nice offer," Min says coolly. "But I've got a better one. You will hand over your ship and all of your cargo. We will pay you with your lives. Argue or fight, and we'll send you and all of your crew on a long walk out an airlock. Got it?" She gives us a cold smile and signals with her hand. The rest of the lights in the room flash on, and we see that we are surrounded by a crowd of about ten fully armed fighters, all looking fierce and dangerous and aiming their weapons at us.

And I remember that blue tintacles mean *trickery* and *lies*.

"Trouble?" Captain Astra says slowly.

"Yes, you are in trouble," Min says, seeming pleased with herself.

"That's not what she means," I tell her, and I shift.

The Hunter moves very fast. I blur from one fighter to the next, crumpling their weapons, deflecting blaster fire away from my captain, Telly, and Electra. In less than two seconds all ten of the fighters are disarmed and the Hunter is back in the center of the room, where I grab Min with a claw around her neck.

HAAAAAAAH, I breathe, and all of her tintacles flinch away as poison drips from my fangs. Her fighters are backing off with their hands raised.

Captain Astra steps from behind the Hunter. "Well now." She gives her laziest smile. "Shall we try this again?" At her side, Telly bares his tusks, looking tough, and Electra stands with hands on her hips, glaring.

"What is this thing?" Min gasps.

I let her go and shift back into my human boy shape. "I'm not a thing, I'm Trouble," I tell her, and start pulling on my clothes again.

"Sorry, Min," the big man says from behind me. "He told me he was a weapon."

Min gives him an icy glare, rubbing her neck where the Hunter grabbed her. "Next time somebody tells you they're a weapon, believe them."

"*And* they have a blackdragon as a pet," the big man adds.

"A *blackdragon*?" Min asks. "Who *are* you people?"

"We're just ordinary traders, trying not to make any trouble," the captain says, with a smile that's meant to be annoying.

" 'Ordinary traders'—hah!" Min shoots back. " 'Operating outside the StarLeague,' you said."

"At least we're not pirates," Captain Astra says. "Like you."

Min says something else, and Telly growls, but I'm distracted because Electra is grabbing my arm and leaning in to whisper in my ear. "Trouble," she says urgently. "She's *not* a pirate."

"Really?" I whisper back, because Min has certainly acted like a pirate, trying to steal our cargo *and* our ship.

"Probably not," Electra whispers. Then she speaks aloud. "Captain Astra."

The captain breaks off her conversation, or argument, whatever, and raises her eyebrows. "Yes?"

"Tintaclodians have a very strong sense of duty and honor," Electra tells her.

"Yeah, I've noticed," the captain puts in dryly.

Electra ignores this. "Min is not a pirate; she's not stealing for the sake of stealing. There's something else going on here."

"Huh," the captain says. "You're sure, Electra?"

At the captain's words, Min jerks around to stare at Electra. Her face goes ashy green and her tintacles fade to gray. "What . . ." She glances at Captain Astra and swallows. "What did you just call this girl?"

"My name is Electra," Electra answers, frowning.

"Your name," Min says slowly, her voice shaking, "is Electra Zox."

When she says this, all of her fighters react, gasping or whispering to each other and crowding closer. I get ready to shift back into the Hunter.

Min holds up a hand, and the fighters go still. Her tintacles are beginning to flush pink with surprise. "My name is Minerva Zox." She goes on, speaking quietly. "Electra, you are . . . you are my daughter."

17

There was a time not too long ago when I was separated from Captain Astra. It was at the end of my mission to rescue the baby shapeshifter. I was floating in space waiting for the captain, listening to the singing of the stars. I knew she was coming, but it was a long wait, and finally the ship appeared and it picked me up.

I am her kid, so when the airlock opened and we were together again, Captain Astra took me into a big, comforting hug and kissed the top of my head, and she was sort of crying with happiness, and so was I, because I was so glad to see her and Reetha and Amby and the rest of my family on the *Hindsight*.

So, you know, I figure that's what kids do when they meet their parents. They hug, and sometimes they cry.

That's not what Electra and Minerva Zox do.

They stand there staring at each other. Electra's tintacles are a muddy pinkish brown, which means she's confused and upset.

Her mother takes a deep breath, as if to steady herself. Her tintacles drain of color and settle on her shoulders. She's completely controlled.

"I—I remember," Electra says slowly. "The StarLeague took me away from you."

"You can't remember," Min says, her voice suddenly cool. "It was twelve years ago. You were a baby."

Electra gulps, and her tintacles flush a nervous orangey brown. "I *do* remember. You cried. Your tintacles were golden with sadness."

"It was a long time ago," Min Zox repeats. "And now you are a StarLeague cadet." She studies Electra carefully.

"I'm not in the StarLeague anymore," Electra says.

Min glances aside at Captain Astra. "You got her out?"

"I got myself out," Electra says stiffly.

"I see." Min crosses her muscly arms.

I'm still waiting for them to start crying and hugging, but I guess Tintaclodians are different from humans. Min has already gone back to seeming cool and in control, and Electra has her arms wrapped around herself. Even her tintacles have pulled in close. It's almost like she's shutting herself away from her mother.

Min takes a step back and points with her chin at the big man who brought us into the room; he's standing behind us with his eyes wide with surprise. "This is Jocko." At her nod he steps into our circle. "Tell them," she says to him.

"Right." With a big hand, he waves at the other fighters. They seem a little dazed from seeing Electra meet her mother. They are all different kinds of people: a few other Tintaclodians, a lizardian, two insectoids, a humanoid with puppy ears and a tail. "All of them," Jocko says in his deep, rumbling voice, "and me and Min, all of us have kids taken by the StarLeague." Jocko reaches up and runs his fingers over the flower tattoo that surrounds his eye and has leaves and curlicues that extend over his scalp. "My child, Rosie." His pink eyes well with tears. "They took him, only five years old."

Electra blinks. "I know him," she says. "Rose. He was in my squad."

Jocko's big face brightens. "He's alive?" he asks eagerly. "Is he all right? My flower! How is he?"

"He's . . . he's a good fighter," Electra says blankly.

Jocko blinks. "Oh. Is he happy?"

Electra's hands clench. "Probably not," she says, and a bite of acid has crept into her voice. She glances at her mother's stony face, and then away again.

I'm not sure exactly what's going on. But I edge closer to Electra so she'll know I'm here, I'm with her.

One of the insectoids pushes forward, her frondy antennae quivering. "One of my daughterssss," she hisses. "Moth like me."

"Maybe," Electra says. "If she was in my class. Otherwise

I wouldn't have seen her. What is her name?"

Before the insectoid can answer, the humanoid with the dog ears and fluffy tail steps closer. He is tall and has a furry face and sad dark eyes. "My child. Drigo, a little boy. Do you know him? Is he all right?"

"Stop," Min says, stepping between him and Electra, who is looking worried. "Back off. She'll answer all of our questions. But first I want to talk to my daughter." She gives me and the captain and Telly a challenging look. "Alone."

18

After we've left Electra to talk to her mother, Captain Astra and I are hurrying through the rusty metal corridors of Dread-knot Station.

"We are *not* leaving Electra here forever," I say.

Captain Astra casts me a worried look as we hurry along, but doesn't say anything.

Telly isn't with us either. He stayed behind to negotiate payment for the *Skeleton*'s treasure, and to start unloading it from our cargo bay onto the Dread-knot so Min Zox's crew can load it onto her ship, which will take it back to their home, a moon that orbits some remote planet.

And Electra is talking to her mother. I *hope* she won't want to stay with her. She might. Kids are supposed to be with their parents. What if she does? Electra is my best friend in the entire galaxy. I don't want her to leave!

But I know what she'd say about that.

One night in our room I was lying in the narrow top bunk staring up at the 147 stars stuck to the ceiling, close enough to touch.

Electra was in the lower bunk. She'd wrapped her tintacles in a headscarf and pulled her blanket up to her chin, and then it was time for our nightly talk, there in the darkness.

"What was your training like," I asked Electra, "when you were a StarLeague cadet?"

"It was tough," she answered. Then she told me that the StarLeague had a military academy on a planet called Apex-9, where it trained kids from all over the galaxy to be good StarLeague weapons, like her. "We had our squads. We barely talked to anybody else. And we never, ever talked about the families we were taken away from."

"Why not?" I asked.

"We couldn't. To survive, we had to focus on what was right in front of us. Anybody lost in the past would be . . . lost." She took a shaky breath. "The cadets were watched all the time by monitors and by spies in our own squads. We were never alone. We were told how to think and how to act, we were punished if we got things wrong. We never had any choice about anything. It was awful."

"But you told me it wasn't so bad." We'd talked about this before, at the very beginning of our friendship.

"It *was* bad," she said quietly. "I just didn't know any better." After a moment she went on. "I didn't know what it was like to be part of a family, and to get to choose what I want to do. Now that I know, I could never go back."

So Electra is staying on Dread-knot Station to talk with her mother, and if she decides to go live with Min Zox on that remote moon, well, it will be awful, but I can't make her change her mind.

Electra gets to choose.

My stomach growls, and as the captain and I reach the hatch that leads to the *Hindsight*'s airlock, I pull a protein bar out of my coverall pocket and unwrap it.

When we go through the airlock and back into our ship, we're met by Reetha.

"Don't tell me," the captain says, holding up a hand. "The StarLeague picked up the energy signal when Trouble shifted, and they're on their way."

"Yes," Reetha says in her deep voice. "Soon."

"*Rats*," the captain curses. "They are persistent."

"Relentless," I put in, through a mouth full of protein bar. We know that from our previous run-in with the StarLeague. They don't give up when they want something, and supposedly Commander Io is even *more* persistent than most. She got her ship repaired quickly, that's for sure.

"Right," the captain agrees. "We'll just have to make this fast." While she tells Reetha that Min Zox's ship is ready to receive our cargo, so we can start unloading, I quickly eat three more protein bars.

"I'm going back onto Dread-knot Station to get Electra," I tell the captain.

She turns to face me, hands on hips. "Trouble," she says, like a warning.

"I know," I tell her. "She might want to stay with her mother. But I have to make sure."

"Cargo," Reetha interrupts, and heads off.

"Coming," the captain calls after her. Then she turns to me again. "All right. Tell Min Zox's people that we should have time to get the cargo onto their ship, but the StarLeague is on its way. They need to load up and get out of here." She points at me. "Make it fast and be careful, all right?"

I nod. "Don't worry, Mom. I will."

Captain Astra freezes, her mouth open.

As I turn, hitting the button to open the hatch to the airlock, I hear her say, half laughing, ". . . *Mom?*"

19

This time, when I enter Dread-knot Station, there's nobody to meet me. The fastest shape I know is the Hunter, so I shift, pause to pick up my clothes, and race through the dim corridors. As the Hunter is zooming along, my stomach gives a rumbling growl. I stop. Hmm. The corridor I'm in is scattered with all kinds of junk—old pipes, some broken boxes, bits of plastic, greasy engine parts . . .

It all looks . . . *delicious.*

The Hunter's stomach growls again; hungrily, I scoop up the junk and chomp it down. Feeling much better, I *whoosh* through the corridors until I reach the big room where we first met Min Zox and her fighters. I shift into my human form and put my clothes back on, wishing I'd brought socks because the metal floor is icy cold under my bare feet.

"Electra?" I call, and my voice bounces around inside the big, empty room.

Another door opens and the humanoid with the puppy ears and tail peers out. Seeing me, he flinches and ducks away again.

It's all right—I'm used to it. Once I've shifted into the Hunter, that's what people see when they look at me: an ordinary kid who is also a terrifyingly powerful weapon.

I cross the room and go through the door into a much smaller room with rusty walls; the big man, Jocko, is there and stops me with a hand on my shoulder. "They're still talking," he says, and points with his chin.

At the other end of the long, narrow room, Electra and her mother are sitting at a table with their heads close together. Min Zox is speaking, and Electra is nodding, *yes.*

I remember that I have a message from my captain. "Jocko," I say to the big man. "A warning. The StarLeague has a ship coming this way. It'll be here soon."

Jocko shrugs and keeps watching Min Zox and Electra, as if he's a lot more interested in what they're saying. "We'll be well away. They can't track us." Then Jocko turns to stare down at me. "Are you one who was taken too, like my Rosie and the rest? Trained by the StarLeague to be a cadet?"

I blink. "Do I *look* like a cadet?"

Surprised, Jocko gives a short laugh. "Nope. What *are* you?"

"I'm a shapeshifter," I tell him. "The StarLeague made me, and I escaped, just like Electra did."

"Escaped," he says slowly, with a glance at the table at the end of the room where Electra and Min now look like they're arguing.

"Yep," I say. Then I remember how persistent Commander Io is, which might mean I'm not as escaped as I think I am. "Well, mostly."

Jocko stares down at me, rubbing the tattoo on the skin of his head. "We—all of us—have children taken by the StarLeague. You know that."

I nod. Yes.

"We all have other children too," he tells me. "To protect them, we made our own place. It's hidden, where the StarLeague military can't find us."

"So your other kids can't be taken away from you," I realize. "But what about the ones like Rose and Drigo and the Moth girl who *were* taken?"

Jocko nods. "We haven't forgotten 'em. We never will."

Across the room, Min Zox and Electra are getting to their feet.

This is when they should hug, I think, but they don't. Electra's tintacles are bright green. Min Zox says something to her in a low voice.

"*Yes*," Electra says intently. "I *know*. I will." Then she gives her mother a sharp nod and crosses the room to meet me.

At the same time, Min Zox calls to Jocko, and they hurry out the other door.

"Electra, what are you—" I start to say, but without even stopping she grabs me by the sleeve. As she drags me out the door and into the big room, I catch a glimpse of her face.

It's the Electra who is a trained weapon. She is a girl with a mission.

20

Electra brings me to the middle of the big
room where Min Zox tried to trick us before. The walls are rusty
metal, and our voices sound hollow and echoey. The air is cold.

"All right, Trouble," Electra says. "Before I tell you what's
going on, you have to promise that you won't tell the captain
what I'm about to tell you."

I'm already lying to the captain about the *shapeshifter bomb*
thing. I feel a frown gather on my face. Can I keep two secrets
from her?

"T, I am your best friend," Electra says impatiently. As she
speaks, her voice gets louder, and the last word echoes around
the big room we're in: *Friend-end-end.* "I need your help with
this," she goes on. "All right?"

"Yes, all right," I say, nodding. "I promise I won't tell the
captain."

Electra leans closer. "My mother told me," she says quickly, "that I have a sister."

She has a sister! This is like me finding out about the baby shapeshifter. It's a really big deal!! What is it the humans say when they're surprised? "Wow!"

"No, not *wow*," Electra says. "T, listen. My sister's name is Miracle, and she's younger than I am. My mother told me that when Miracle was two years old, the StarLeague came back and they took her away, just like they took me."

"Oh no." I take a shaky breath. "That's terrible."

"I think that's why she's like that," Electra explains. "My mother. Why she seems so . . ."

"Not huggy," I say.

"Right. It's because she lost *two* children," Electra goes on. "I think she can't be motherly to me, not really, until she gets both of her daughters back."

"But—" I start to say, when I'm interrupted.

The door to the big room creaks open and Telly pokes his head in. "Hey, you two," he calls. His deep voice echoes and booms around the room. "Cargo's loaded and we're out of time. Captain Astra says we're out of here in five minutes."

"We're on our way," I tell him, and he nods and leaves. "Let's go," I say to Electra, and head for the door.

She doesn't move. "I'm not coming," she says.

I spin back to face her. "What?"

"Trouble," Electra says, "my sister is in training at the StarLeague academy. There are a lot of Tintaclodians there.

We've never met, but I think I know which one she is. She's my sister, and I have to get her out. I'm going to Apex-9, the planet where the cadet training academy is, and I'm going to rescue my sister and bring her back to our mother."

"No," I say without thinking. "Electra, no." It's too far away. I don't want her to leave. "This is not a good plan."

She straightens and gives me a steely glare. "T, it's what *you* did, when you went to rescue the baby shapeshifter."

"That's true," I say, trying to make up reasons for her to stay, not go. "But you said you never wanted to go back to the cadet academy. You said it was awful."

"It *is* awful," she says through gritted teeth. "And that's why I have to get Miracle out of there."

"All right," I say slowly. She is my best friend, and she's going into danger to rescue her sister. "But I'm coming with you, just like you came with me to help rescue Donut."

"You are *not*," Electra says firmly. "Think about it, T. I'm going to the StarLeague academy. It's where I grew up; I know the place, and I know the people."

"And *they* know *you*," I interrupt. "They know you're not a cadet anymore. They'll throw you into a level-four military prison!"

"Oh *really*," Electra says, straightening, stiffening her spine, snapping out her words. "Even though I was kidnapped by a third-rate pirate captain on a tin-can ship? Yes, it took me a few months to escape, but I am *Cadet Electra Zox*, reporting for duty!"

I stare at her, wide-eyed. It's the Electra who first came aboard our ship, the grim, determined Dart pilot who had a number, not a name.

She relaxes and one of her tintacles waves at me, and she's herself again. "They'll believe me, T. It's the StarLeague. They *want* to believe me, because they trained me to be completely loyal, practically from birth. They'll put me right back into training, because they can *use* me. I'm not a person, T, I'm a weapon, remember?"

I nod, because they made me to be a weapon too.

"And you can't come with me because you, Trouble, are very good at being yourself, and terrible at pretending to be a StarLeague cadet." She quirks a smile at me. "Am I right?"

"You're not wrong," I admit. During the baby shapeshifter rescue, I tried pretending that I was a cadet, and my disguise lasted about ten minutes before General Smag figured out who I was.

"Good." Electra takes my arm and pulls me toward the door. "You have to hurry and get out of here. Don't tell the captain what I'm up to; she'll waste time and try to stop me. I'm going to signal the nearest StarLeague ship to pick me up here, and—"

"Electra!" I interrupt. "That'll be the *Arrow*." And I do *not* want Electra and Commander Io talking to each other.

"Maybe," Electra says impatiently. "The *Arrow*, or another StarLeague ship, what does it matter? I just want you and the *Hindsight* to be far away from Dread-knot when it gets here."

Far away. I feel an emotion welling up in me. She's really going to do it. She has a plan, and she's leaving. "Electra," I say sadly. "The galaxy is so big."

"I know." She reaches out and takes my hand. "But I have to do this. Say goodbye to everybody for me, and take good care of Donut, all right?" Then she grabs me by the shoulders, turns me around, and pushes me away. "Now go, Trouble. *Go.*"

21

Reetha meets me at the *Hindsight*'s airlock. I ran the whole way in my human form, so I'm panting as I come through the hatch and hit the button to seal it behind me.

"Electra," Reetha says. Her golden eyes are fixed on me.

"She's—" I say, catching my breath. "She's not coming."

A moment later there's a *clunk* and a *thunk* and the ship has left the station.

Reetha is still staring at me.

I stare back at her.

The problem with Reetha is that more than anybody else, she sees me—not just the human boy shape, or the Hunter shape, or whatever other shape I take—but *me*. Her golden eyes are so keen that she probably already realizes that I'm not telling the truth about something.

But I promised Electra. I won't tell what she's up to.

Without saying anything I turn and head for the mess-room.

The captain is there, sitting at the head of the table talking to Telly, who has a computer tablet in front of him. Fred is there too, and so is one of the Shkkka.

Reetha brushes past me in the doorway and goes to lean against a wall with her arms crossed. She hasn't stopped staring at me.

The captain looks up and gives me a nod, then frowns. "Where's Electra?"

"She's not coming," I say. This much is true.

"Rats," the captain curses. "She wanted to stay with her mother?"

Here comes the latest lie.

Way back when Captain Astra first learned the truth about me—that I was a shapeshifter *and* that I could take the Hunter form—she was ready to toss me out the airlock, and I cried for the first time. My tears tasted salty, and also like sadness.

Lies taste different from misery. Lies taste like licking the floor in the galley after I haven't cleaned it in a while. Nasty and gritty and ashy.

"Yes," I lie. "Electra is staying with her mother."

"*What?*" Telly asks, frowning.

"She said to tell you . . . to tell everybody . . ." I gulp, and the next word comes out as a whisper. "Goodbye."

"I was afraid of that," the captain says, getting to her feet and opening her arms. She wants to comfort me, but instead of going for a hug, I stand there in the doorway. I should have told her the truth about what Commander Io said to me. Is it too late? But then I'll end up telling her the truth about Electra, too, and I *can't*!

And . . . and . . . and Electra is *gone*.

I'm so confused, I feel like dissolving into a puddle of goo!

"You all right, Trouble?" the captain asks.

I blink. "Yes," I say. Another gritty, nasty, ashy lie! "No," I add.

"Can we get on with the meeting?" Fred interrupts. Both of his eyestalks glare at me. "I have to get back to the bridge to recheck our course."

"Yeah, all right," the captain says with a worried frown at me; then she sits down. "Go ahead, Telly."

"We cleared a profit on the deal," Telly says, giving me a sympathetic nod and then glancing at his tablet. "Fourteen thousand." That must be how much money we made from selling the *Skeleton*'s supplies to Min Zox and the others.

"Good," the captain says with a satisfied nod. "We'll head for Janx Station. You'll all get paid—"

"—finally," Fred puts in grumpily.

Ignoring him, the captain goes on. "And I," she says with a sudden grin, "will be paying off what I owe on this ship. We'll be free and clear."

"Huzzah!" Telly says, and twitches his ears so that the little golden bells on his earrings tinkle.

Reetha gives an approving nod, and even Fred looks less cranky.

Then they all get up from the table and head out to their duties. "Sorry about Electra," Telly says with a pat on my shoulder. "We'll all miss her."

"Yesss," the Shkkka says, and pats my cheek with one of her antennae.

Reetha doesn't say anything, but she gives me a steady *I know you're lying* look as she goes out the other door with Fred.

Leaving me with the captain.

"Come over here," she says, pointing at the seat next to her.

I go over and sit down.

And then I slide under the table and shift into my dog puppy shape. The dog puppy is the first form I remember taking. Brown fur, floppy ears, sad eyes. The puppy can't talk, so she can't tell any more lies. But the puppy wants to howl, already missing Electra.

The captain bends to look under the table. "Oh, kiddo," she says with a sigh. Then she lowers herself to the floor, sitting cross-legged. "Come here."

I edge closer, lying down next to her with my nose on my paws.

"Trouble," the captain says softly. "Do you remember one of our midnight conversations, when we talked about leaving people behind?"

I remember.

Space is big, she told me. *People travel with you for a while, and you may like them—or even love them. But things happen, and you never see them again. That's just how it is, Trouble.*

"You know I will never leave you behind, right?" she asks.

Yes, I know. She's my captain—she's my *mom*—and I'm her kid. The tip of my dog puppy tail gives a small wag.

"Electra has gone back to her family, which is a good thing for her," she says. "We'll try to make sure you see her again someday, Trouble, but the galaxy is such a big place. She was your first friend, and she was a good one. But you have to understand. It's likely you'll never see Electra again."

My dog puppy shape trembles. The captain rests a hand on the top of my head. "Sorry, kiddo," she says. "That's just how it is."

Another pat and she gets stiffly to her feet and goes out.

I stay in my puppy form, feeling sad. But I'm not confused anymore.

I know how it is for the captain. She's like a blackdragon—she likes the dark emptiness between the stars. She thinks that sometimes you have to leave people behind, even if you love them.

That's not how it is for me.

Electra is my best friend.

Not *was*. She *is*.

22

It's easier to keep the lies out of my mouth if
I don't have to talk to anybody, so I stay in my dog puppy
shape while the *Hindsight* travels to Janx Station. We leave the
empty part of the galaxy where the Dread-knot was and head
for the galactic center, where there are lots of bright star systems and stations and people and ships zipping along busy
trade routes.

Donut is in the stripy pillow shape. Somehow its yellow
and purple don't look quite as bright as usual. Maybe it's unhappy because Electra left. I curl up next to it on the lower
bunk that was Electra's and listen to the sad songs of the blackdragon, which is still wrapped around the end of our ship.

I'm worried about Electra. She stayed on Dread-knot, and
by now she's been picked up by a StarLeague ship, probably by
the *Arrow*. What if Commander Io tells her about shapeshifter

bombs? And what if Commander Io doesn't believe Electra when she tells her she was kidnapped? She might be on her way to the academy on Apex-9, but it's also possible that she's on her way to a military prison. Electra is amazingly brave and determined, but even she must be scared right now, and I'm scared for her.

Captain Astra says we get to choose, but I'm completely certain that there are some things she would never let me do, and running away so I can help Electra is one of them. Something I've learned since being a human boy most of the time, and having a family, is that sometimes the people you love don't know what's best for you. Sometimes, even if you're a kid, you have to decide what to do for yourself.

And maybe I'll have time to figure out what, exactly, Commander Io meant when she said that it's *not completely true* that I'm a weapon, and *not in the way you think*. And what she meant when she said that I'm a *bomb* about to *explode*.

So I've decided what I'm going to do.

I'm not going to leave Electra behind.

Janx Station is one of the brightest spots of the galaxy.

As our ship approaches, the screen in the mess-room shows the station—a huge, lumpy shape. Maybe long ago Janx Station was a simple ring, but it's been built onto with no planning at all. It's lopsided, with a huge junked ship welded onto one side of it, and an asteroid embedded in the other, and scaffolds jutting out into space for unloading cargo, and random docks for ships to pull into. All around it, hundreds of ships float like gleaming jewels, and shuttles are zooming back and forth. It's a busy, exciting place that people visit from all over the galaxy.

On the *Hindsight*, the crew is getting ready to go onto Janx Station. They're planning to go shopping because Telly wants to buy some more plants, and then he and Reetha will visit a place called a *bar* to drink *beverages*, and Fred wants to enter a contest for the strategy game we like to play after dinner in the mess-room. The captain is going to a *bank*, which is a place that buys and sells money—I don't understand that part of it—to pay off what she owes on the ship, and then we're all supposed to meet at a restaurant to celebrate. *With food that is not noodles and cheese powder*, the captain says, with a wry glance at me.

I've shifted into my human boy shape and am in my room putting some things into a bag that I found in one of Electra's drawers: a big supply of protein bars and the StarLeague coverall uniform that I used when Electra and I sneaked onto General Smag's ship. I look around for Donut, but it's not in the room. Hiding, maybe? I check under the bed, but it's not there, either. I wonder if I really need to find it, to take it with me in case the *bomb* thing turns out to be true.

The door pings, and then opens, and it's the captain. I turn to face her, hoping she can't see the half-full bag on the bed behind me.

"Yeah, I'll be right there," the captain is saying to somebody farther down the corridor. She gives me a smile. "Hey, Trouble. We've docked. I'm off to the bank. Here's some money."

She tosses me a chip, which I catch. "Money?"

"There are all kinds of things on the station that you might want to buy," she explains. "Like, for example, food. Go and explore, eat things, and have fun. But meet me at the station office in two hours. It's on the second level, section B-32. We'll have some forms to fill out."

I don't get it. "What forms?"

Her smile widens. "Remember what you called me the other day?"

I think back, past the lies and the secrets. "Mom?"

"I realized something when Electra decided to stay with her mother," she says. "We need to make it official." She points at me. "My kid." She points at herself. "Your mom. Don't be late." And then she spins and heads off down the corridor.

Rats. The captain is going to be very unhappy with me when I miss the special dinner and the official Mom forms.

Once everybody's gone, I finish packing my bag, put the money chip into my pocket, and make my way to the cargo bay, to the shadowy corner where the rats have their den in a box with a hole in the side. I crouch next to it and say, "Hey, rats."

When the rat with the gray muzzle comes out of the box, I ask her for a favor. It's a big one, and I offer the money chip that the captain gave me in exchange, because that's how money works.

The rat takes the chip in her little pink paws, so I know the rats will do what I need them to do so I can help Electra rescue her sister.

With that settled, I head for the outer hatch where our ship is connected to Janx Station.

Holding my bag, worrying about what's happened to Donut, I step out of the *Hindsight* and into a wide corridor that is crowded with people rushing around, and colorful and loud with music and 3D advertisements.

Leaning against a wall on the other side of the busy corridor, as if she's been waiting for me, is Reetha.

23

Seeing me step out of the *Hindsight*, Reetha doesn't move; she just waits for me to come across the busy, noisy corridor—dodging hurrying people and small robots that zip along near the floor—to talk to her.

Reetha's arms are folded across her chest. She gazes down at me with steady golden eyes.

She knows exactly what I'm up to.

"Are you going to try to stop me?" I ask.

Reetha doesn't say anything; she just keeps staring at me.

"I'm going to help Electra," I tell her.

She nods.

"I'll be careful," I say. "Tell the captain not to worry, all right? And . . . and *you* don't worry about me either," I add. "If you worry. Maybe you don't . . ." I fall silent. What does she *want*?

A group of insectoids pushes past us, and I step closer to Reetha to get out of their way.

"*Skeleton*," she says in a low voice.

"The *Skeleton*," I repeat. "Where we got the treasure. What about it?"

"Signal," she says. "Suspicious."

I frown. I'm not sure what she's talking about.

She huffs out a frustrated breath. "*Skeleton*. Why. Us."

"I don't know," I say, still not sure what she's getting at.

Reetha unfolds her arms and points at me with a green-scaled finger. "Why. Us." Then she points away, down the busy corridor. "Now. Go."

All right, Reetha! I'm going!

I'm not in a huge hurry, because the rats have a lot to do before I can actually start. But I have to be ready. I head out into the busy, crowded, loud, colorful station. The first thing I do is find a humanoid-designated bathroom. Jostling past a pair of people with purple skin and pointed ears, I go in so I can change out of my regular clothes and into the StarLeague uniform.

I take a second to think things over. I just passed humanoids with purple skin and pointed ears; they had webbed fingers too, and droopy tentacles around their mouths. The way my shapeshifting works, I could easily shift into that form—or a Tintaclodian, or a lizardian, or anything—and be completely in disguise when I go to Apex-9 to help Electra rescue her sister.

But I like my human shape. Sometimes it feels normal, and sometimes completely strange, but of all the forms I've taken, my human boy shape is starting to feel the most comfortable, the most like *me*.

That's settled, then. Trouble Hindsight, new StarLeague cadet, is a human species.

Finding an empty cubby, I go in and close the door behind me. I open the bag and reach in.

And I pull out a crinkly handful of protein bar wrappers. I take out the StarLeague uniform and peer into the depths of the bag. There's nothing else in there, just crumbs. I close the bag and hold it up, eyeing it suspiciously.

The bag just sits there in my hand, looking like a bag.

But it's not a bag, it's Donut.

"You ate my protein bars!" I accuse it.

It keeps pretending to be a bag. And then it burps.

For a moment I consider taking Donut back to the ship, but even though I think Commander Io is wrong about it being a bomb, Donut will cause trouble if I leave it behind, so it might as well come with me. Plus it likes Electra a lot more than it likes me. I think.

With a shrug, I change out of my Trouble clothes and into the short-sleeved black coverall with the StarLeague logo on the front. My human hair is a little long for a cadet, but it should be all right.

When I pick up the bag again, Donut has added a strap so I can carry it over my shoulder.

Now I have to wait for a rat.

Staying in the least crowded corridors because I don't want to accidentally run into anybody from the *Hindsight,* I make my way to the main docks, where the biggest, most important ships come in. I lean against a wall next to a busy restaurant and watch a huge screen high on the wall across from me; it's showing a news report about some StarLeague ship that's gone missing at the edge of the galaxy. It's not very interesting, so I turn to watch all kinds of people walking past—humanoids with elaborate hairdos and fancy clothes and skin that is brown or pink or deep blue or green, and lizardians glaring at anyone who gets in their way, and groups of insectoids scurrying along, and methane-breathers wearing masks, and tall storkers screeching at each other, and now and then a StarLeague officer trailed by hyper-alert soldiers.

I know I should feel nervous about the *Arrow* and persistent Commander Io.

I know I should be feeling sad about leaving my captain, who is, at this very moment, heading for section B-32 so we can fill out the Mom forms. What will she think when I don't show up?

I should be sad about leaving the rest of my family too, and worried about the blackdragon.

And I do feel sad and a little worried . . .

But I'm also excited and happy that I'm going to see my best friend soon, and help her rescue her sister. There's all kinds of adrenaline zipping through my human body, and I can barely keep still as I'm waiting. Come *on*, rats!

At last I feel a *tap-tap-tap* against my foot; looking down, I see a small gray rat.

Finally.

It leads me to the end of a narrow, trash-strewn alley. I crouch, set down the Donut-bag, then shift into my rat form.

The rat that has come to meet me is a station rat, not one from the *Hindsight*. In its pink paws it has an ID chip.

As you probably know, every person in the galaxy has an ID chip implanted in them when they are born. *You* have one, I'm sure. It's so that whenever you step on or off a station, like this one, or onto a planet, the StarLeague knows where you are, and they have information about *who* you are too. I was never born, I was made, and the StarLeague doesn't think I am a person. So I don't have an ID chip.

That's usually a good thing, since my friends and I aren't exactly law-abiding StarLeague citizens. But if I want to help Electra, I have to have a chip.

For rats, computers are like mazes—rats are very good at figuring them out, and also doing sneaky things with them. When the rat hands me the ID chip, it means they were able to get into the computers and set everything up for my plan. Thanks, rats!

When I shift back into my human boy shape, I'm careful to shift around the ID chip so it's in me, right at the back of my neck. Then I put on the StarLeague uniform, pick up the Donut-bag, and head for the docks. Time to find the ship that will take me to the StarLeague military academy on Apex-9.

24

Let's see, the ship I'm looking for is in dock-
ing space X14-34. Jostled by hurrying people, I make my way
along the docks, past restaurants and shops on one side, and
cargo pods and the outer hatchways of docked ships on the
other. The air is cold and smells like engine oil and humanoid
sweat and like delicious spicy things cooking. My stomach
growls, and I regret giving away the money chip that the captain gave me because I could have used it to buy something
to eat.

"I wish you'd left me some of the protein bars," I say to
Donut, who is still in its bag shape.

Donut, of course, doesn't answer.

Then I spot it. At docking space X14-34, an open hatch-
way. A soldier in a StarLeague uniform is stationed out front,
standing at attention. He's a humanoid with folds of pale pink

skin over his face, a wide mouth, and an extra fold of skin for a nose; his small black eyes are staring straight ahead.

I go over to him. "Hello," I say cheerfully. "Is this the StarLeague troop transport ship *8-29-70*?"

The black eyes swivel down to me. "Who wants to know?" he asks in a bored voice.

"New cadet Trouble Hindsight reporting for duty," I tell him. *Reporting for duty.* Sounds very cadet-like, doesn't it?

Are you wondering what a cadet *is* exactly? What I know is that a cadet is not a regular soldier. Some of the cadets are like Electra and her sister—taken from their families when they were babies because they were identified, probably through their ID chips, as being extra-talented, good cadet material.

Other cadets are kids who are in regular StarLeague schools and do well, so they are transferred, sent to the cadet academy to be trained as weapons. That's the kind of cadet I am, or so the StarLeague computers think.

The soldier pulls a device out of his pocket. "ID chip." I lean my head down, and he scans the chip in the back of my neck, then checks the readout. Thanks to the rats, the StarLeague computers think there really is a Cadet Trouble Hindsight. "You're in cabin 16, deck B," the soldier says. His eyes flick to Donut. "Is that your only baggage?"

"Yep," I say.

The black eyes glare at me. "Yes, *sir*, you mean."

"Yes, sir," I repeat.

"Go on in," the soldier says.

"Thanks!" I say, and go up the ramp to the ship's hatch, and inside.

The corridors of troop transport ship *8-29-70* are painted gray and are bare except for door labels and signs. As I walk along with the Donut-bag over my shoulder, I pass soldiers who are wearing the same black coverall uniform that I am, and weirdly, they all walk the same way, and they all keep their eyes facing forward. They're not kids, but adults, different species from all over the galaxy, which means they're taller or shorter or have tintacles, or pointy ears, or four arms, or various colors of skin or hair or scales, or whatever—but their StarLeague training has tried to make them all the same. I wonder why. Why is sameness a good thing for them? As I go along, not one of them says *hello* back to me. One or two of them break out of their straight-ahead stares to give me a look, as if I'm the one behaving strangely when *I* say a friendly hello to *them*.

At cabin 16, I push a button, the door whooshes open, and I go in. It's a long room with a narrow corridor between stacks of bunk beds.

A big lizardian soldier—not a cadet, a grown adult—rolls off one of the bottom bunks and stands to block my way. His StarLeague uniform is stretched over bulging muscles. Another lizardian and a humanoid with yellow skin and fuzzy hair are standing behind him, watching, and a Tintaclodian peers out of one of the upper bunks to see what's going on.

"Hello!" I say, and add, "Trouble Hindsight, reporting for duty." It worked well last time, anyway. I wonder if I should salute, or something. "I'm on my way to the special cadet training academy on Apex-9."

"Whatever, kid," the big lizardian says. "Hand it over."

I blink. "Hand what over?"

"That bag," the lizardian says, and points at Donut.

"No," I say.

The lizardian takes a menacing step toward me. "I said. Hand. It. Over."

"And I said no!" I say, and hold my ground. I feel the Hunter shape stirring. But no. I can't shift here. As I realize that my human shape isn't even remotely dangerous or scary, the lizardian grabs me by the front of my uniform and jerks me off my feet; then he wrenches the Donut-bag away from me and drops me onto the floor.

"Give that back!" I say.

"Make me," the lizardian sneers, holding Donut high up, where I can't reach it.

And oh, I have never wanted anything in my entire life as much as I want to shift into the Hunter. It would roar ferociously, and poison would drip from its fangs, and it would move so fast to take Donut back again. Can you imagine how the lizardian and everyone else in cabin 16 would screech and scream and scramble to get away?

But no. You're a human boy, Trouble, at least for now, I tell myself. Get used to it.

"All right," I say, gritting my teeth. "Fine."

"Top bunk," the lizardian says, pointing.

Yep. That's a top bunk, squeezed in just below the ceiling. With a ladder leading up to it.

The lizardian leans closer. "Get in it," he orders.

Oh. All the others in the room—all grown-up soldiers, not cadets—stare as I climb up the ladder until I get to the bunk at the very top. It's so tight a fit that I have to wedge myself in.

I lie there staring at a ceiling that is only a few inches above my nose and has no glow-in-the-dark stars stuck to it. My stomach growls.

So. This is the StarLeague.

It could be worse, don't you think?

25

By the middle of the night, Donut has found
its way back to me. It's in its stripy pillow shape snuggled up to
my side when I wake up in the dark. My fingers can feel that it
has added a silky fringe along its edges.

"Hello," I whisper to it. My stomach growls loudly.
"*Shhhh*," I tell it. The room is dark and stuffy and smells like
lizardian farts and humanoid sweat and somebody's stinky
feet. A sound woke me—it must have been the ship leaving
Janx Station. We're on our way to Apex-9. And stops on other
stations and planets too, but hopefully we'll arrive at the cadet
training planet quickly.

For a while I lie there in the dark feeling hungry. There was
no dinner; all the soldiers just climbed into their bunks not long
after I came aboard. It's still hours until breakfast. Assuming
they *have* breakfast in the StarLeague. Maybe they do. Kaff,

and scrambled eggs with cheese powder, and donuts . . .

Growl, growl, growl goes my stomach.

Maybe I could . . .

GROWL.

Gah. That was loud enough to wake every soldier in the room. So hungry, have to do something about it. Quickly, I shift into my blob of goo form. In my bunk there's a blanket and a small pillow that is not Donut. My blob of goo form extends a pseudopod, grabs the pillow, and eats it. Mmmm. Delicious. Then I shift back into my human boy shape—making sure the ID chip is where it's supposed to be—and slither into my clothes.

There. That's better.

I lie there in the dark for a bit longer. If I were on the *Hindsight*, I'd get up and go to the galley. Captain Astra would come in and I'd make eggs with neon cow-cheese powder for a midnight snack, and we'd have a long, interesting conversation. What was it she called it, that hollow feeling that isn't hunger when somebody you love isn't there? Oh, right. I *miss* my captain. My mom. She's probably not very happy with me right about now . . .

Then I realize that the soldier in the bunk below me is talking. She's whispering to the soldier in the bunk across from her. *Deep Dark*, I hear. And *Soon*.

Quietly, I slide over to the edge of my bunk and poke my head out, listening keenly.

"—any mission out there," one of the soldiers, a humanoid, whispers to the other.

"What do you think it is?" the other asks.

"A threat, my commanding officer said. She wasn't specific. But they're calling up a lot of soldiers. Have you ever seen a troop transport as full as this one?"

"Never," the other whispers. "And the officers seem nervous."

"They know something," the humanoid says.

"More than we do," the other answers.

And then they fall silent. I wedge myself back into my own bunk. Huh. Something's going on in the Deep Dark at the edge of the galaxy.

Nothing to do with me, though.

The rest of the trip to Apex-9 takes four days, and the lizardian soldier, whose name is Mek, is the only interesting thing about it. He stomps around and is mean to everyone, and he's wonderfully surly when he realizes that the Donut-bag returned to me, and he tries stealing it two more times. We're let out of our room to an exercise area for an hour every day—I do push-ups and sit-ups, just like Electra taught me—and for two meals. The ten of us from cabin 16 sit together at a long table and eat quickly, just like the soldiers at the other crowded tables. The soldiers, I notice, sit straight, and they all chew their food ten times before swallowing it. There's no talking. That may be because there is an officer standing at the end of the room, so they're all on their best soldiery behavior, unlike when they're in our cabin. I'm the only kid, the only new cadet headed for Apex-9.

At dinner on the second day, I'm next to Mek. "What is this?" I ask, poking my dinner with my fork. It's a gray blob that tastes like salty gray plastic. At breakfast it tasted like sweet gray plastic.

"Loaf," Mek tells me. Then he reaches over, stabs my loaf with his fork, and shifts it to his own plate.

My stomach growls. I'll have to find another pillow to eat later. The problem with pillows, though, is that they are filling but not very nutritious. "What I wouldn't give for a bowl of stew right now," I say, pushing away my empty plate.

The others look at me out of the corners of their eyes and eyestalks. Their mouths and mouthparts keep chewing.

"Loaf is terrible," I go on. "On my ship I was the galley boy, and I made hot stew every chance I got. Vegetable cubes, protein cubes." I look around the table, and they're all pretending I'm not saying anything. "And that delicious brown sauce, you know?"

With a low growl, Mek shifts what's left of the loaf back onto my plate.

"Thank you!" I say as the rest of the soldiers stare, surprised, I guess, that he gave it back.

"If he's chewing on that," he says in a low voice, "he'll shut up."

"True," I say, and take a big bite of the horrible loaf.

Three more days of loaf, the narrow bunk, half-hearted menace from Mek, six more pillow snacks stolen from the other bunks, and we finally get to Apex-9. An insectoid soldier comes into our room and tells me to head for the main hatch. I gather up Donut, unwedge myself from the bunk, and slide down the ladder to the floor, where I'm met by Mek. He looms over me, all muscly and scary.

This time, if he tries to take the bag, I *will* have to fight him, because I can't leave Donut on this ship.

"Listen," he says, and with a scaly finger he reaches out and pokes me roughly in the chest. "Keep your head down."

I blink. What does that mean, *Keep your head down*? Is he trying to give me advice?

I see him eyeing my Donut-bag, so I edge past him and get out the door before he can grab it. Then I poke my head back in. "Thanks!" I say.

"Keep your head down at the cadet academy, little human," Mek repeats. "Or they'll bite it off for you."

There won't be any actual biting off of heads, I hope. But it *is* advice. Probably very good and helpful advice for somebody like me.

26

If you're used to being on a spaceship or a station for your entire life, going down to a planet is a deeply weird experience.

I mean, space is *huge*, right? But mostly we're not *in* space, we're inside a ship that's in space, and the ship is a very small place, with floor, walls, ceiling, normal gravity, even temperature, and the constant, steady hum of the ship's engines. Ships are very homey and safe . . . and *same*-y.

I've only been on a planet once before.

On the planet the air was moving around in strange ways, which is called *wind*. There were prickly tiny plants called *grass* that you could actually step on. There was a star called a *sun*, which was close enough to be warm and light everything, which is slightly terrifying, if you think about it. And there was the *sky*, which was huge and colorful and full of puffs of water vapor called *clouds*.

Like I said, deeply weird.

A pilot flies me in a shuttle down to the surface of Apex-9. We go from the darkness of space to the rattle-and-shake of hitting the atmosphere, and then into a controlled glide as the shuttle adjusts to the planet's gravity. We fly lower, but for a long time the only thing I can see out the window is dull gray cloud.

Suddenly the shuttle shoots into sunlight, dazzling my eyes as I peer out. We're coming in low over rocky pieces of land that poke up into the sky—mountains. They're covered with . . . really big grass? Dark green, pointy, tall . . . Oh— trees! On the tops of the mountains there are no trees, only white stuff that might be ice, but it looks like cloud, too. Ice-cloud. The sky over it all is brilliant blue.

The shuttle makes a wide turn over the endless dark green of the trees, and I see, laid out below me, the academy. It is a huge stone building jutting from the edge of a cliff. Its massive outer wall is crossed by regular rows of narrow windows and topped with sharp metal spikes. Behind that is a central court-yard and a square tower also edged with spikes with a landing pad on the top of it. As we come closer I see that beyond the main building are trees and land that slopes up into a ring of steep mountains as sharp as teeth.

Not exactly a friendly looking place.

The shuttle slows, and then with a lurch we drop down to

land in the courtyard. The pilot doesn't say anything as I pick up the Donut-bag and step off. As soon as my feet hit the stone ground, the shuttle door snaps shut behind me and the pilot lifts off, buffeting me with a blast of wind, leaving me standing alone in the middle of the courtyard facing the central tower.

The huge walls of the academy building enclose the courtyard and rise high enough to block the sunlight, casting dark shadows across where I'm standing. The air is icy cold, but not nearly as cold as outer space. A light wind called a *breeze* is blowing. I hold up a hand to feel the breeze against my skin, and my human body gives a shiver.

Near one of the shadowed inner walls of the academy is a row of four kids—cadets, I mean—a lizardian, two humanoids, and an insectoid—dressed in the same short-sleeved coverall that I am, and for some reason they've taken off their boots, so their bare feet must be freezing cold on the icy stone of the courtyard, but they're just standing there at attention, staring straight ahead, with their breath coming out as puffs of steam.

Before I can go over to say hello, an older, black-uniformed soldier comes out of big double doors in the tower. He's tall, and he has white skin, and he's so thin that at first I think he is made of bones on the outside. Catching my eye, he nods.

I sling the Donut-bag over my shoulder and cross the cold stone courtyard, passing out of the shadow until I'm standing on the sunny steps just below him.

"Trouble Hindsight," I say, squinting up at him, "reporting for duty."

Silently, he studies me for a long moment. "Yes," he says at last. His voice is hoarse and sort of slithery. "I am Monitor Gorget." In bony hands he's carrying a short club made out of metal. He turns and uses it to point at the doors. "Go in."

I go up the steps and through the big doors into a stone entryway with a wide hall beyond it and stone stairs on either side. A few cadets in black coveralls cross the hall. They march in step, not talking. The air is warmer than outside, but it still feels heavy and cold, as if the stone is soaking up whatever heat there is. The monitor follows me in and points up the stairs. "My office," he says. "The door at the top."

I start up, then stop and turn back, a few steps above him. "Those four cadets in the courtyard. They looked awfully cold. What were they doing out there?"

Monitor Gorget studies me again. Then in his raspy voice he says, "You, Cadet, will find out soon. *Very* soon."

27

The stairs go up and up to a landing; there I
find a door made of some shiny brown material. I look around
for a button to make it open, and there isn't one; there's just a
round metal knob on one side. I push it, and nothing happens.

"Turn it," says a hoarse voice from behind me.

I flinch away, startled. Monitor Gorget is standing right
behind me, tall and bony. He came up the stairs so quietly that
I didn't hear him. He leans past me and grasps the knob on the
door and turns it, and the door clicks, and instead of sliding up
like a normal door, it swings open. I step in with the Donut-
bag over my shoulder and Gorget following.

The room is made of bare stone with a tall window-slit
on one side; on the other is a square hole in the wall with an
actual fire burning in it. I stare. On a ship, fire is the very
worst thing—I mean, you never, ever, *ever* have open flame on

a spaceship. Looking more closely, I see that it's burning *wood*. One of the most valuable substances in the entire galaxy, and they've lit it on fire for warmth! I spin around and look at the door I just came through. It's wood too! There's also a desk made of wood at the other end of the room.

Then I realize. Wood comes from trees. This place is surrounded by trees. Wood isn't as valuable here as it is out in deepest space, where there aren't any trees for trillions of miles.

Monitor Gorget steps past me and goes to the desk, where he sits and starts typing something into a tablet. After a while he looks up, studying me. "Cadet Trouble," he says in his raspy, slithery voice. "Cadets use only first names here."

"And numbers," I put in, remembering when Electra first joined us on the *Hindsight*.

"Only when on a mission," Gorget says. "You are a transfer from the humanoid Earth system. We don't get many humans who qualify," he goes on. "You must have friends in high places."

Friends in low places, I think. Rats. Rats are the friends who got me here.

"Or perhaps you have . . . hidden talents," he says.

"I do," I tell him.

He eyes me for a very long, heavy moment.

"I do, *sir*," I correct myself.

Monitor Gorget gets up from his chair and leans on the table, staring down at me. I think he does it to make me feel small. It works. "Some advice, Cadet."

"I know," I tell him. "Keep my head down. I will try to. Sir."

His eyes narrow. "Insubordination will not be tolerated. Cadets are expected to observe behavior protocols at all times. Immediate obedience to orders is expected. Punishment is swift and not to be questioned. Understood?"

I don't know what *insubordination* or *protocols* are, but I can guess. Don't talk back. Actually, don't talk at all. March in step, stand at attention, say *Yes, sir*, chew every bite of food ten times, and be a good little weapon of a cadet. "Yes, sir," I say, putting a little soldiery snap into my voice. I can do this if it means helping Electra rescue her sister.

"You are assigned to Double-star Squad," Monitor Gorget tells me.

Double-star Squad. If the rats did their job with the computers, it'll be the same squad that Electra is in, which means I'll be seeing her soon, assuming she really is here and not in a StarLeague prison somewhere. That would be a whole other problem for me to deal with.

Don't worry, I'm not stupid. If Electra is here, I'll have to pretend I don't know her. But she's my best friend, and we're both weapons. We'll figure out a way to work together to get her *and* her sister out of this terrible place.

28

Our meeting is over, so Monitor Gorget leads me down the stairs and out to the main hall. The cadets we pass watch me out of the corners of their eyes and eyestalks, but nobody stares. I follow Gorget up another set of narrow stairs and then down a long corridor with wooden doors on both sides. We follow this around one corner and then another, and along another corridor until we stop at an unlabeled door.

"Double-star Squad's ready room and bunk," Monitor Gorget says, then steps past me and, without knocking, opens the door.

Inside there's the sound of rushing footsteps and chairs being pushed back, and then Gorget steps aside and I go in.

The room is all gray—stone ceiling, stone floor, stone walls—with no window and no fire. The air is damp and chilly. In the middle of the room is a wooden table with six wooden chairs around it; on the surface of the table are five tablets, all carefully lined up. Five cadets are facing the door, standing at attention, eyes forward.

One of them is Electra.

I'm *so, so* glad to see her. Thanks to the rats, everything is going according to plan.

Electra doesn't react when I step into the room, and her tintacles are bound up in a head-wrap, so I can't tell how she's really feeling.

"Squad Leader Electra," Monitor Gorget says. With his metal club he pushes me forward. "A new cadet assigned to your squad. See that he is outfitted, informed of the protocols, and ready to attend instruction in the morning."

"Yes, sir," Electra snaps.

"Any faults to be reported immediately, Squad Leader," Gorget adds.

"Of course, sir," Electra says.

With deeply set black eyes, Gorget carefully studies each cadet in the room. He steps over to the table and inspects the tablets; with a bony hand he reaches out and adjusts one of them, lining it up precisely with the edge of the table. "Yours, Cadet Drigo?" he asks in his raspy voice, and points with the metal club.

"Yes, sir," one of the cadets answers. He's a humanoid with a furry puppy face, droopy mouth, one folded-over ear, and sad eyes. Drigo. One of the children taken from Min Zox's people.

Gorget stares at the cadet for a long moment; then he nods, spins on his heel, and leaves the room.

None of the cadets move.

Electra, still at attention, turns toward me. Her face is blank, but I can tell that she's very, very annoyed with me right now. "Name?"

"Cadet Trouble," I tell her. Without the Hindsight part of my name, because cadets don't use last names here.

"You address me as 'Squad Leader,' Cadet," she orders.

"Yes, Squad Leader," I say dutifully.

"At ease," she says, and the other cadets relax. Electra points them out. "Cadet Drigo." The droopy, sad one. He nods, but doesn't say anything.

"Cadet Rose." This one is the son of Jocko, who works with Min Zox, which means he's also one of the cadets taken from his family as a child. He's big, hairless, pink-eyed, pink-skinned. He nods too.

"Cadet Sekka," Electra says, pointing at an insectoid, a mantis with a green carapace, triangular face and bulbous eyes, and antennae that arc gracefully from her forehead. She twitches one of them at me.

"And Cadet Tyran." The last cadet is a slim green-scaled lizardian with black eyes; a wide, lipless mouth; and a forked tongue that darts out as if testing the air.

"Hello," I say to all of them, and give them a half wave and a smile. They're all cadets, true, but they're also kids, like me.

"Cadet Trouble stood at ease before ordered, Squad

Leader," Tyran says in a slithery voice. "That is a fault."

"I am aware," Electra says briskly. "A fault noted to Cadet Trouble," she adds. Tyran leans forward and makes a note on one of the tablets.

I think I just got into trouble without realizing it.

"So, Cadet Trouble," Electra says, still in her Squad Leader voice. "Double-star is the best elite tactical attack and infiltration squad at this academy. What skills do you bring to our team?"

"I'm very dangerous, Squad Leader," I tell her.

At that, she blinks, and I know she's remembering the time she told me that my human self is more dangerous than my Hunter self. She said my human self took over the *Hindsight*, which I didn't really, but they did let me stay instead of spacing me or turning me over to the StarLeague.

"I have hidden talents," I add.

"I'm sure," she says acidly.

"Squad Leader!" the lizardian cadet interrupts.

"Yes, Cadet Tyran?" Electra answers.

"Permission to take Cadet Trouble to Stores to pick up his kit."

The faintest frown creases Electra's brow. "Permission granted."

"Thank you, Squad Leader!" Tyran says. He flicks a black-eyed glance at me. "Come along, Cadet Trouble."

I follow him out. Without speaking we head down the corridor. As we go on, making lots of turns and going up and down stairs, I try to march in step with him, but I'm not very good at it. As we turn a corner, he remarks, "That's a fault, Cadet Trouble. It will be noted."

I don't even know what I did wrong.

"I think you will find," Tyran sneers, "that our training here is a lot more difficult than it was on whatever rat-bitten planet you're from. You'll probably fail quickly and be sent home in disgrace."

"I'm a lot more likely to be sent home in a spaceship," I tell him.

He adds more sneer to his other sneer, and we keep walking. Finally we reach a room with a counter across the front. A soldier in the usual black uniform comes over and picks up a tablet.

"New cadet kit for this one," Tyran says, pointing at me with a slim green-scaled finger.

"Human," the soldier says with a nod. "We have his size ready. Wait a moment."

I watch him go into the room beyond, which contains rows of shelves with supplies stacked on them. He goes to one and pulls out a coverall and some other things.

"I already have a bag," I call out to him, and put the Donut-bag on the counter.

He flicks me a glance, but doesn't respond. He goes to a few more boxes and pulls out a few more things, which he brings to the counter and stacks in a pile. Coveralls, boots, socks, a warm-looking jacket, a tablet, and some other things, and I'm not sure if Donut is big enough for all of it to fit inside. But when I pick up the Donut-bag, it's helpfully made itself bigger. Carefully, I put all the things into it, hoping Donut won't decide to eat it all. Then I really *will* be in trouble.

"Thanks," I say to the soldier, who gives me an odd look.

When I turn away from the counter, Tyran is gone.

Looking for him, I step out into the hallway and notice something that I should have noticed before.

The academy building is huge. There are hundreds, maybe thousands of rooms and corridors, classrooms, gathering halls, dining halls, offices, enough rooms for lots of cadets of all ages, maybe ten thousand in all.

That's a lot of kids who were taken from their parents. Not all of them—some are kids who did well in school and were sent here, kids who maybe *want* to be cadets.

Anyway, it's a lot of rooms and corridors, and nothing is labeled. All the corridors are exactly the same gray stone; all the doors are the same plain wood.

I have no idea where I am or how to get back to Electra's squad's rooms.

And I realize. Tyran volunteered to bring me here and now he's left me alone on purpose.

This is a test.

29

What I need is a rat.

Or . . . to *be* a rat.

As I told you, rats are very good at mazes. I'm absolutely certain that there are rats at the academy and they have no trouble at all finding their way around this place.

I don't even know which way Tyran and I came from, so I pick a random direction and start walking . . . and worrying.

Here's the problem. Electra was right—I am *not* good at pretending to be a cadet. I think Tyran the sneerer already suspects that I'm not what I'm pretending to be. So I may not have much time to help Electra find her sister and then escape.

Hurrying, I turn corners and climb stairs until I get to a deserted stretch of corridor.

Quickly, I set down the Donut-bag and shift into my rat form. I sniff along the bottom of the wall where it meets the floor, and it's not long before I find a rat scent mark. Oops. I've gone completely the wrong way.

Shifting back into my human form, I fling on my coverall, pick up Donut, and head back the way I came, running whenever there's nobody around. I get oriented and go up some stairs and along a corridor. Two cadets march past, eyeing me as I hurry along, out of breath. As soon as they go around a corner, I shift. The rat scent markings are easy to find again. I'm on the right track. I head off, having to shift twice more to find my way again. Finally I go up some stairs, down a long corridor, around a corner, fourth door on the left. I shift again, making sure the ID chip is where it's supposed to be, get dressed, pick up Donut, and run.

At last I skid to a stop in front of Double-star Squad's unlabeled door, and without knocking, I turn the knob and go in. The squad is sitting at the table with their tablets in front of them; they all look up, surprised, as I burst into the room.

"Hah!" I say, pushing the door, which closes behind me with a loud *slam*. I grin at them. "Good try, Tyran," I say, "but I made it back."

Electra is sitting at the end of the table, and my grin widens as I see her give the faintest flicker of an exasperated eyeroll.

"That's a fault," Tyran complains, pointing at me.

"What fault, exactly?" Electra says dryly.

"He . . ." Tyran flicks out his tongue, tasting the air. "He has obviously run all the way back here, and—"

"Did you *see* him run, Cadet Tyran?" Electra interrupts.

"No," Tyran admits. "But he's out of breath, and . . . and . . . he's *happy*."

"Not a fault, as far as I know," Electra says without looking at him.

"You're just mad that I passed your test," I say to him, and set the heavy Donut-bag on the floor.

"*Sahhhh*," Tyran hisses at me.

"Enough," Electra snaps. "Cadet Trouble, stow your things in the bunk room, and do it quickly. We have mess call in six minutes."

Mess call means dinner.

At last!

Before we step out into the hallway, Electra has the other five of us line up for an inspection. "Straighten your collar, Cadet Trouble," she tells me. And before Tyran can say anything, she adds, "It's his first day, Cadet Tyran. Let it go."

I see the other cadets give each other wide-eyed looks at that. Uh-oh. Electra's being too nice to me.

Then she has us march out the door and into the hallway, where we join other squads marching to dinner.

The dining hall is huge, with a high ceiling, and it would be loud and echoey if anybody said anything, but along with one hundred other cadets we march in silence to a counter where we're each given a plate with our dinner on it.

Oh *no*. The dinner is rubbery gray loaf. With a hungry hollow ache in me, I miss stew. I miss cheesy noodles and eggs and cake and donuts. I miss things that *taste* like something to eat, not like gray plastic!

Still, I'm ravenously hungry, so I carry my plate in front of me to a long table with benches on either side, and like the other cadets in Electra's squad I place my plate on the table and then sit down. Nobody starts eating; all one hundred cadets in the mess-hall just sit there staring straight ahead. My stomach growls. I can't wait to start chewing every bite of this loaf ten times.

Monitor Gorget and some other monitors in black uniforms are going around the hall. At some tables they tap a cadet on the shoulder with their short metal clubs, and the cadet gets to their feet and stands there, eyes forward, at attention.

When he gets to our table, he stops near me and I feel the club tap me on the shoulder. I glance around the table. Tyran is looking smug, so I know it can't be good. Monitor Gorget is standing right behind me. The club taps me again on the shoulder, harder this time. Slowly, I get to my feet.

"Four faults, Cadet Trouble," Monitor Gorget says in his raspy voice. "You lose your dinner privilege."

"No *dinner*?" I gasp, turning to face him. All the cadets that the monitors tapped must be in trouble, so they have to stand at attention while everybody eats. But why me?

The metal club pokes me in the chest. "Another word, Cadet," he barks, "and you'll go without breakfast in the morning."

"But I only had two faults," I protest.

Behind me I hear Electra give the faintest unhappy sigh.

Monitor Gorget leans over me. Everyone in the mess-hall is staring straight ahead, but I know they're all keenly aware of what's going on. The metal club pokes me in the chest again. "You, Cadet," he snaps, "have just earned yourself some time on the punishment parade." He steps back. "Come with me."

I figure arguing is only making it worse, and a real cadet would obey, so I follow him out of the mess-hall. We go down a corridor until we reach the main entrance hall, and then he leads me out the wide main doors to the courtyard where the shuttle dropped me off just a few hours ago.

Remember when I arrived, there were four shivering cadets standing barefoot out there? They were on punishment parade, it turns out.

Now the courtyard is empty. The sky was blue earlier, but it has turned a weird orangey color, which I assume is normal for a planet. The air is cold.

When we get to the middle of the courtyard, Monitor Gorget stops and faces me. With his metal club, he points to my feet. "Boots and socks off."

Brrr. I bend and take them off, and stand up again, my feet bare.

"Do not move from this spot," Monitor Gorget orders, "until I return for you." He looks me up and down. "At attention," he orders. I straighten. Then he leans close, and in his grating voice he adds, "You see, Cadet? I told you when you arrived that you would soon find out what those cadets were doing. Although I have to admit that I did not think you would find out on your very first day." Then he turns and stalks away, going through the main doors, leaving me standing alone in the middle of the courtyard.

He's not wrong. I didn't think so either.

30

The punishment parade means me standing barefoot, in short sleeves, in the middle of an icy-cold court-yard until Monitor Gorget decides I've been out here long enough.

Hopefully that's before I freeze to death.

I'm a shapeshifter, but when I'm in my human boy shape, I'm an actual human boy. Still, I don't usually feel the cold as much as a human would, the same way I don't get as tired or need as much sleep. But right now I'm very, *very* hungry, and I do eat a *lot* more than a real human kid ever would, and be-cause I'm so hungry it makes me feel colder and tireder than I normally would.

But it's probably not as bad for me as it is for the regular cadets.

This is not a good place for kids.

The cold from the courtyard stones seeps into my bare feet. An icy breeze blows, and little chill-bumps prickle over my bare arms. My breath comes out in puffs of steam. Overhead, the sky goes from orange to pink, to gray, to darker gray. The planet is turning, I realize, turning away from its sun. The sun is a source of heat, which means it's about to get colder. It's about to be *night*. Brrr. I start to shiver. My stomach growls.

I really don't like this very much.

I eye my boots and socks, and think about eating them. But then I'd have to explain how I lost them. So I stand there trying to ignore the annoyed growls coming from my stomach.

In a little while, the sun has completely disappeared, and the sky is dark. One by one, stars appear; slowly, the darkness gathers and even more stars glitter and shine. It's outer space coming all the way down *here* to the planet. Standing there, I gaze upward. Somewhere out there is my ship, and my captain, and my family. Amby's out there too, with their family. They're all far away, but they can see the stars of our galaxy just like I can. I think about how my captain—my mom—loves the darkness between the stars, and I wonder. If I listen hard enough, could I hear the stars singing?

As I'm gazing up into the deep, velvety black, a faint, distant star blinks and then goes out.

I stare. Stars don't just disappear, not even the ones at the farthest reaches of the galaxy. It was just the faintest pinprick of light. Maybe it's still there and I just can't see it. I rub my eyes and squint.

And as I'm watching, another star blinks out, swallowed up by the darkness.

For a long time I stand, watching, but no more stars disappear. There's only that blank place, like a dark stain, in a tiny corner of the sky. Eventually I stop shivering. I've gotten so cold and hungry that everything feels sort of distant. I could shift into another form, one that wouldn't feel the cold at all, but somehow I can't be bothered.

After a while, wisps of cloud creep across the night sky, blotting out the stars. The clouds grow heavier. The air gets colder and damper, and then I see bits of white whirling through the darkness. One of them lands on my face. It's a soft touch, and then icy cold. It must be a tiny piece of frozen cloud. I wonder what it's called.

The white cloud-stuff continues to fall all around me, until it's piled up on the ground, and also on my shoulders and covering my feet like a white blanket, only one that's made of ice. I come back to myself and start to shiver for real, and I begin to worry that maybe Monitor Gorget isn't going to come back at all.

But at last, there's a gleam of light from the main door, and a knife-sharp shadow crosses the courtyard, crunching over the frozen cloud-stuff until Monitor Gorget is standing in front of me.

"Hello," I say through frozen lips.

"Need another hour out here, Cadet?" he asks.

"Definitely not," I say.

"Another hour it is," he says, turning away. "Do not move from that spot."

Rats! I forgot to say *sir*. A fault, Cadet Trouble!

By the time another hour passes, I've given up on standing at attention, and I'm crouching on the freezing stones, curled into a ball, as more frozen cloud pieces fall onto my head. This time he sends Electra out to get me.

"You idiot, T," she says as she reaches me.

I'm too cold to talk.

She reaches down and pulls me to my feet. A glance over her shoulder to check if we're being watched, I guess, and then she pulls me into a hug. I lean into her, and feel warmer, and happier, and start to shiver again. "H'lo, 'Lectra," I manage.

"Of *course* you came," she says, pulling away and steadying me with a hand on my shoulder. "I *knew* you would. I wish you hadn't, but I'm glad you did." She bends and picks up my boots and socks.

"C-C-Commander Io believed you," I say.

"Io?" Electra asks. "Oh, on the *Arrow*. Yes. I barely talked to her. I told her that I'd been kidnapped by the *Hindsight*, and she didn't ask any questions, she just dropped me here on her way to another station."

Good. Commander Io was in a hurry to catch up to the *Hindsight* on Janx Station, so she couldn't have talked to Electra about shapeshifter bombs.

"Have you f-f-found your sister?" I ask.

"Yes," Electra says quickly. She looks sharp and serious,

like a cadet. "My mother thought I wouldn't be able to do it, but I *have*, and I'm going to get my sister out of here. I'll fill in the details when I can, but there's a lot more than that going on, and we have to get you warmed up right away. Come on." She takes my hand and starts pulling me across the courtyard.

And then everything is a blur as she brings me through the night-dark corridors back to Double-star Squad's rooms, where the others seem to be asleep. There, she shoves me into a bunk and covers me with blankets, and shushes me when I try to tell her that the bag I brought my stuff in is really Donut. She leans over to whisper in my ear. "Shift if you have to, T, to get warmed up. I'll be on guard, and I'll look after Donut. It'll be all right."

31

In the middle of the night, I wake up in my human boy form, shivering and shaking.

Nightmare.

Not surprising.

It was the same old dream about the military weapons lab. But this time there was something different. One of the scientists who was studying me pulled down her mask, and it was somebody I knew. It was the kind, wrinkly face of Commander Io.

There in the darkness I sit up, wrapping my blanket more snugly about me. I wonder if Io really was there, in the lab. She definitely knows more about me than I know about myself.

I sit there for a while, my thoughts a jumble of nightmare and stars blinking out and missing my mom. Slowly, my human heart settles and I start to feel sleepy again. And then I hear the faintest muffled sniffling sound.

The Double-star Squad bunk room is narrow, made of stone, of course, and has a stack of three wooden bunks against two of the walls. At one end is a narrow door that leads to a bathroom for use by any species; at the other end is a narrow door leading to the ready room with the table and chairs in it.

There's a little light coming from the open bathroom door. Everything else is quiet and dark. I glance across the room and see a blanket-covered lump that is Electra sleeping in her bunk, with the Donut-pillow nestled against her back.

Then I hear a low whimpering noise. It's coming from overhead.

I'm in the bottom bunk. Over me is Tyran, and in the top bunk is Drigo.

Quietly, I unwrap myself from my blanket and climb carefully up the ladder. At Tyran's bunk I pause.

All I can hear is a faint *sssssss*. Tyran breathing, asleep.

I climb the rest of the way to the top bunk, Drigo's. The puppy-faced kid is curled at one end of the bed, and he's sound asleep, but he's whimpering. His long nose is twitching and his fists are clenched.

I know what this is. Just like me. Bad dream.

"Drigo," I whisper.

He whimpers again, still caught in the claws of his nightmare.

"Drigo," I say again, and reach across to him.

As my hand touches his shoulder, he jerks awake, and for a moment we stare at each other.

"You were having a bad dream," I whisper.

He takes a ragged breath.

This time when I pat him on his shoulder he doesn't flinch. "You're all right," I tell him.

"Oh," he whispers in a trembling voice. "Are you going to report me?"

"Nope," I assure him. I really wish I could tell him that I've seen his father, who misses him and wants him to come home. But I can't.

He takes another shaky breath. "I'm all right."

I pat him on the shoulder again and quietly start climbing down to my own bunk.

I know he's not all right.

None of the kids at this academy are all right, even the ones who chose to be here, but especially the ones who were taken from their families.

As I fall asleep, I think about how I'm here on this planet to help Electra help her sister to escape. And maybe Jocko's son, Rose, if he wants to go. And now that I know Drigo has nightmares, I'm sure he would like to leave too. I'm going to help them do it.

In the morning I wake up as the other cadets start stirring. From my warm nest of blankets I see the mantis cadet, Sekka, come out of the bathroom already dressed and looking every inch the perfect cadet.

"*Finally*," big, pink-skinned Rose complains. "I hope this time you left us some water to wash with, Sekka."

Sekka ignores him, using a foreleg to primly clean the length of her antennae.

Pushing the blankets back, I climb out of bed and pull on my coverall. Electra is sitting on the opposite bunk, wrapping up her tintacles. "Good morning," I say to her.

Tyran's scaly green face peers down from the bunk above mine. "Good morning, *Squad Leader*, you should say."

I smile and say a cheery "Good morning, Cadet Tyran!"

Tyran hisses at me.

"You two," Electra says as she finishes tying up her tintacles. "Do not interact in any way for the rest of the day, Cadets, or you'll both be given a fault."

"Yes, Squad Leader," I say at the same time that Tyran does.

Drigo climbs down from the top bunk.

"Good morning," I say to him.

He blinks, and then says in a low voice, "Thank you."

I know what he means. Thanks for waking him up from his nightmare. "It was no trouble," I say.

My answer surprises a smile out of him. Then he frowns again. "You missed dinner last night," he says worriedly. "You must be very hungry."

"I'm fine," I say, because when I was climbing down past Tyran's bunk I shifted into my blob of goo form and ate his pillow, which was about as tasty as the loaf any of them had for dinner, and much more filling. Despite the pillow, I'm very hungry for breakfast.

Sekka is waiting by the door looking perfect and annoyed. "Idle chatter is not permitted," she says in her clicky insectoid voice.

I give Drigo an apologetic smile and head for the bathroom.

Once we're all washed up—no hot water, brrr!—and have made our beds—Tyran complains about his missing pillow and glares suspiciously at me—and are dressed and inspected, Electra leads us down to the mess-hall, where we eat rubbery loaf, chewing every bite ten times. When we've returned our plates to the serving counter, we go back to our rooms, where Electra tells us to put on our warm jackets. It's time for physical training—that means we're going outside to run around until we're tired.

While we're gathering our things, I hear lop-eared Drigo whispering worriedly to Rose. It sounds like they don't usually train this hard, and he's wondering if a new mission is about to come up. Maybe that's why he had a nightmare.

"Quit worrying," Rose whispers back to him. "There's nothing we can do about it if there is. Just obey orders and keep your head down, will you?"

And Drigo agrees. "I will."

I will too. I'm really good at keeping my head down. Yep.

32

A bunch of trees clumped together is called a
forest. There is forest all around the enormous academy building, leading up to the steep gray stone of the mountains. There
are trails through the forest, and that's where we run. Other
squads are running too, in single file through the trees, moving like silent black shadows against the white of the bits of
frozen cloud that fell out of the sky last night.

I follow Electra as we run along a narrow path leading up-
hill. The air is crackling with cold, and it goes into my human
lungs and makes me feel full of energy. I bound along looking at the trees, and the chunks of rocks that stick out of the
ground, and the bright blue sky.

Planets are amazing! So many different things to see and
smell and listen to, like the crunch of our running feet on the
path, and the sound of wind in the high branches of the trees.

Now and then I catch a glimpse of an actual wild animal—a flying feathery one or a small brown furry creature. And there are smells—it must be the trees that smell so fresh and green and *alive.*

The path winds back and forth and gets steeper, and I can see Electra's breath puffing out, and ahead of her the other four in our squad: Drigo, then the perfect and not-very-nice Sekka, then Rose, then sneery lizardian Tyran, who keeps glancing back at us. At last we get to a high place where the trees thin out and the steepest face of the mountain begins. We stop for a second to catch our breaths.

From here we can see the academy in all its huge stoniness, with the tall tower at its center, and the mountains and forest all around. "What is this stuff?" I ask, bending down to touch some of the shredded cloud ice that covers the rocks beneath our feet.

Electra snorts. "It's called *snow*, Cadet."

I pick up a pile of snow. It starts to melt in my hands. I bend down and pick up some more and shape it into a ball. "Look!"

"Never been on a planet before, Cadet Trouble?" Tyran sneers.

"Just once," I answer, taking a bite of the ball of snow I just made. Cold! "And there wasn't any *weather*." I grin at him and hold out the snowball. "Want to try it?"

Tyran gives me a mean look. "Sure." Then he takes three steps away, stoops, picks up some snow, molds it into a ball, and hurls it straight at me, so the snowball explodes across my face.

"Ow," I say, wiping snow out of my eyes.

"*So* sorry, Cadet Trouble," Tyran says with fake sweetness.

"You're about to be even sorrier!" I say, laughing, and bend to pick up a pile of snow to dump on Tyran's head, when I realize that Sekka is watching me very intently, and her antennae are twitching. Oops. I drop the snow and wipe my cold, wet hands on the front of my jacket. Having fun and being happy aren't very cadet-like, and I don't want to make Sekka—or anybody—suspicious.

"Enough arguing," Electra interrupts. "Let's go."

"Yes, Squad Leader!" Tyran snaps, being such a good and proper cadet that it really makes me want to shove a handful of snow down the back of his neck.

With a last sneer at me, he starts running down the path we came up. I follow the rest of the squad.

It turns out going downhill is even more fun than running up. It must be the planetary gravity, pulling us down. Wheee!

Electra, a step ahead of me, slows until we're ten paces behind the others. "Pretend you're tired," she says over her shoulder.

I slow and take a few stumbling steps.

"Keep going," Electra yells at the others. "I'll stay with Cadet Trouble."

The others in our squad keep running, and Electra slows until she's jogging alongside me. "We don't have long to talk."

Ahead, Tyran looks back at us. "I think Tyran is spying on us," I note.

"Oh, he definitely is," Electra says, "and reporting to Monitor Gorget."

"Really?" I ask.

"There's always one spy in a squad," Electra says as we jump over a small branch lying across the path. "That's just how it is."

"I can't believe pieces of cloud fall onto the ground here," I say, pointing at the snow. "Is that normal for a planet?"

"Shut up, T," Electra snaps. "I have a lot to tell you and only about five minutes until we have to catch up to the others."

"Shutting up, Squad Leader!" I say cheerfully. Running is a lot of fun; I'm surprised they let the cadets do it.

"Seriously, just listen," Electra says. Ahead of us, the path curves and we lose sight of the squad. Electra slows and grabs the front of my jacket, and we stand facing each other, panting clouds of steam into the cold air. "I found out more about my sister," she tells me. "She's the leader of a junior tactical squad. But my ID chip tracks all my movement," she goes on, "so I haven't been able to contact her."

"I can help with that," I say.

"Good," she says, and we start walking. As we come around the turn in the path we see that Tyran has slowed down; he's only about ten paces ahead of us. "Rats," Electra curses. "There's more, T," she says quickly, starting to jog again, pulling me along with her. "If we're going to get her out,

we have to hurry. There's something else going on, and—"
She breaks off as we get closer to Tyran, who is looking suspiciously at us.

Something else going on? Does it have to do with what Drigo is worried about—a new mission?

I'll have to figure out a way to talk to Electra again. Soon. Without Tyran-the-spy overhearing us.

Unfortunately, the only way I can think of is for me to spend another ice-cold night in the courtyard.

33

The funny thing is, I get faults without even trying.

I get the first ones at the end of our run as we're jogging with the other squads into the courtyard, where Monitor Gorget is waiting for us with his hands behind his back, holding his shiny metal club.

"Do we get to do that every day?" I ask as Double-star Squad forms up into a line.

"Unfortunately," big, pink-skinned Rose answers without moving his lips.

Somehow Monitor Gorget is looking straight at me when I laugh. He points with his club. "Two faults to Cadet Trouble," he says, "for failure to maintain protocol." No talking, that means, and especially no laughing.

"Noted, sir," Electra replies stiffly.

Our squad marches inside, dropping off our warm jackets in our bunk room and then marching to our classroom, yet another unmarked door in a row of doors along a stone corridor.

The classroom contains rows of desks, fifty in all, lined up precisely; there are three slitted windows that let in beams of light that slant across the shadowy room. The cadets from a bunch of different squads file in without talking, and each stands at attention next to a desk. Electra points to the desk next to hers, and I stand there. After a silent five minutes of watching bits of dust swirl around in the beams of sunlight, the teacher comes in from a side door. She is wearing a black StarLeague uniform and has all-seeing eyestalks and muddy gray skin and a pinched-up mouth, just like Fred, our navigator on the *Hindsight*.

She sees me immediately. "We have a new student," she says in a biting voice, setting a tablet on her own desk at the front of the room.

"Yep," I answer. "Cadet Trouble." And then I add, "Reporting for duty!"

My words seem to echo in the silent room.

"A fault to Cadet Trouble," the teacher says sharply, "for failure to maintain behavior protocol."

"Noted, Instructor," Electra says without looking at me.

The teacher paces down the aisle between the desks until she's standing in front of me. Her eyestalks look me up and down. "In this class, Cadet Trouble, we study strategy and tactics. Do you have any knowledge of this subject?" She says it as if she suspects that I don't.

But thanks to Electra, I do! "Yes, Instructor!" I say happily. "Strategy is the big plan during a battle. Captains make strategy. Tactics is who gets killed or hurt while carrying out that plan." I point to the other cadets in the room. "That's us."

At my words there's an actual stirring from the other cadets, and a few gasps. "Silence!" barks the instructor. Her eyestalks glare around the room. "Two more faults to Cadet Trouble," she says. "And you will stand at attention for the rest of the class as an example to the others."

An example of *what*, I wonder.

But I stay on my feet without arguing while the other cadets sit down and take out their tablets and get to work on a strategy problem.

For a while I stand stiffly at attention, staring straight ahead, like a good little cadet, but then I get distracted. The ceiling of the classroom is very high overhead, with heavy stone beams that go across, and it's covered with ragged, dusty webs made by long-dead spiders. As I watch, the webs flutter, and a small shape swoops across and disappears. I tilt my head to see better. It's a flying planet creature! A bird! Tiny and brown, it flits to the web, gathers some in its beak, and disappears again. It must be making a little house up there.

For a second I have the strongest urge to shift into a tiny bird shape so I can swoop among the spiderwebs too.

When I stare straight ahead again, the instructor is

watching me from her desk. "Another fault for Cadet Trouble," she says sharply. "When you are ordered to stand at attention, you *stay* at attention."

That's six faults, and it's not even lunchtime!

"And," she adds, "a fault to Squad Leader Electra, for failure to maintain behavior standards in her squad."

Oops. I risk a glance aside at Electra.

She pretends I don't exist. "Yes, Instructor," she raps out. "Noted."

Later, as we're standing in the corridor outside our next classroom, Electra at attention beside me. "T," she whispers, "what are you *doing*?"

"What's the record," I whisper back, "for the most faults in a single day?"

I swear, I can hear Electra's teeth grinding together from where I'm standing.

During the class, I get another fault because my stomach growls so loudly that it startles me and I drop my tablet on the floor. This is good, because the more faults I get, the easier it will be for me to get to Electra's sister.

Before lunch, we stop off at our ready room to leave our tablets and pick up our blasters and warm jackets because we have weapons practice later. While we're there, Monitor Gorget materializes at our door for a quick inspection, and

I get another fault for having a non-regulation pillow on my bed. Donut, of course, in its purple-and-yellow stripy form.

In case you've lost count, that's eight faults.

When Monitor Gorget leaves, Tyran gives me a smug look, and I figure he's the one who told about the pillow.

As we're strapping on our weapons, the furry-faced Cadet Drigo edges up to me. "Be careful," he warns in a low voice. "There are worse things than the punishment parade."

"Really?" I ask. "What's worse?"

"The quiet room," Drigo whispers. "They put you in a tiny room. It's dark and it's cold and they don't let you out for a long time. And there are rats."

"Rats!" I exclaim.

"Shhhhh," Drigo says with a sideways look at Tyran, who is of course listening in. "Yes, rats. They come up out of the drain in the floor. It's horrible."

I wonder what sad-eyed Drigo did to be sent to the quiet room. For him, it must have been pretty bad, although if I know rats, they were probably just trying to help.

For me, the quiet room sounds like exactly what I need—a place for Cadet Trouble to stay while sneaky shapeshifter Trouble goes to find Electra's sister.

34

After lunch, which I spend standing at atten-tion with my stomach growling after getting a tap on the shoulder from a grimly pleased Monitor Gorget, our squad has weapons training. It's also strategy and tactics and exercising, all rolled into one.

I don't have to keep up my disguise for much longer, but still, I'm determined to be a good cadet weapon and make nobody suspicious. I'll try to remember to say "Yes, sir!" a lot, and never smile.

Monitor Gorget loads the six of us onto a hover-sled and drives us miles out into the forest, down winding paths and then even farther, where there are no paths, only trees and snow. More snow is falling from the sky, and we're all wearing our warm black uniform jackets. Finally he stops the hover-sled and tells me to get out.

"Yes, sir!" I say, and jump onto the snow-covered ground.

Then Monitor Gorget tells our squad that it's the five of them against me. The idea is that I get a ten-minute head start, and the rest of the squad has to hunt me down.

"*Hunt* me?" I ask. "And shoot me?" Wow. "How do any of you cadets survive your training?"

Monitor Gorget gives an annoyed sigh. "The blasters are on a less deadly setting. If you're hit, Cadet Trouble, you won't die."

Prim Sekka puts in, "The blasters fire an extremely painful and paralyzing bolt." She sounds very pleased about that, and strokes her own blaster as if she's imagining shooting me with it. "Then you will lie in the snow squirming in agony until Monitor Gorget comes to find you."

"Where's *my* blaster?" I ask.

Turns out I don't get one. That's all right. Sekka must not have been paying attention when I told the other cadets that I have hidden talents.

I bounce on my toes, excited. "What if I beat everybody back to the academy building?" I ask.

Monitor Gorget frowns at me. "You won't, Cadet."

"Nobody ever has," Tyran says with a flick of his forked tongue, earning himself a stern look from Gorget.

"Can I start?" I ask, turning to an opening in the trees. Part of the challenge here is going to be finding my way back before dark, because there's no path out here, only blank snow.

"Go!" Monitor Gorget says, and off I run.

The tricky thing about snow is that when you run through it, you leave a clear trail of footprints.

Still, I run as fast as I can until Monitor Gorget and the rest of Electra's squad are far behind me.

Then I stop, shift into the Hunter, and eat a big boulder, and also part of a fallen tree, and some snow.

Feeling much better, I shift back into my human shape, put on my coverall and jacket again, and climb a tree. The trees in this part of the forest grow so closely together that I can jump from one to the next. See? No path in the snow to follow! Finally the next tree is too far away, so I drop from a lower branch and start running again.

Electra's smart, and so is her squad, so they'll figure out my trick quickly. But now I've got a really good head start.

I could shift to a faster shape, like the Hunter, but even with the falling snow to cover my path I'd leave suspicious-looking Hunter footprints. Plus I want to do this as me, as human boy Trouble.

I peer ahead through the falling snow, through the bare tree trunks, and I catch a glimpse of a black-clad shape racing through the trees, and I drop to the ground, holding my breath so the puff of steam doesn't give me away. It's Rose, keenly alert. He scans the area and runs on.

I climb to my feet and run in the other direction.

On the way out here we drove in a big arc, going around

a huge rock outcropping—almost a cliff—that blocks the way back to the academy. The expected return route would be to go around, the same way we came.

Instead of heading to the right, I go left, toward where I think the cliff must be. Shortcut. Picking up the pace, I bound through knee-deep snow, dodging trees, jumping over branches.

At last I reach the base of the cliff. It looms above me. The sun is starting to set, so the cliff face is nearly black in the fading light, and crusted here and there with snow and ice. There are plenty of handholds. I start up.

The rock of the cliff is cold, and my fingers quickly go numb. The cracks and shelves that I'm using to climb up are slippery with ice. Panting, I pause, looking up. Halfway. And I'm starting to feel tired and hungry. A chunk of rock comes off in my hand, and without thinking I pop it in my mouth and swallow it. I edge sideways along a crack in the rock so I can reach the next handhold.

My foot slips on a patch of ice, and I cling to a crack in the cliff face until I know I'm not going to fall. If I did, it's a long way down, and I'd have to shift as I fell and that would feel like cheating, but if I didn't shift, I'd probably break both my legs.

Maybe this wasn't such a brilliant idea after all.

Gritting my teeth, I start climbing again until at last I pull myself over the top.

Made it!

I get to my feet and race along the top edge of the stony

cliff, kicking up plumes of snow with every step. To my left looms the outer wall of the academy, grim and gray through a curtain of falling snow. Ahead, on the other side of a line of trees, is a long open slope leading up to the academy's main gate and the courtyard, and if I can get into place in time . . .

The forest thins out. I find a lone tree halfway up the hill the rest of the squad will be climbing. With numb fingers, I shape snow into balls, packing them tightly, until I have a nice pile of ammunition. I leave it behind the tree, skidding down the slope to a boulder, where I make more snowballs. Then I hide, and wait. The pounding of my heart settles. I start to shiver.

Heh. *Tactics* are about to happen to Electra's squad. Grinning with anticipation, I peer around the boulder. Just emerging from the forest are the shadowy shapes of the squad, all sleek and deadly in their black uniforms and jackets. They'd do better by wearing white, I think. Black makes them clear targets in the snow.

Oh, a good thought. Quickly, I strip off my jacket and turn it inside out so the pale-colored lining is on the outside.

The five other members of Double-star Squad are racing up the slope; they're huffing clouds of steam as they run. Tyran is in the lead.

Perfect. Picking up a snowball, I take aim and fire.

I have time to see the snowball splatter across the front of Tyran's jacket, and I've already thrown the next one, which clips Sekka across the back of her head. She shrieks and drops her blaster, and then the next snowball hits broad, unmissable Rose, who trips and goes facedown in the snow.

Staying low, camouflaged in my inside-out jacket, I cackle evilly at the sound of the squad's outrage and race to the pine tree where I left the other pile of snowballs. Seizing one, I throw it hard at Electra, who is looking for me behind the boulder, and then I launch three more, all of them finding their targets.

"There he is!" I hear Electra shout, and I lob one more snowball and run laughing up the slope way ahead of them.

The rest of the squad hasn't caught up by the time I stagger into the courtyard and bend over with my hands on my knees, trying to catch my breath. The air has gotten colder and the snow is as fine as dust, blowing across the stones, whirling up into icy spirals. There's no color anywhere, just the steep gray stone walls, the darkening sky overhead, the white snow falling, and the dark paving stones that have been swept clean by the wind.

Hearing a shout, I straighten and turn to see Electra and her squad trotting into the courtyard, panting.

Electra lopes over, grabs me around the neck, and gives my hair a rough tousle. "Very tricky!" she says, laughing, and Drigo and Rose join in, looking surprised.

Facing the rest of the squad, I give them my biggest, happiest, most triumphant smile.

But then the smiles drop off their faces and they snap to attention.

Slowly, I turn, and there is Monitor Gorget. As usual, he slithered up so quietly that none of us realized he was watching. He studies us long enough for the cold of the courtyard to seep into me. I begin to shiver.

"You cheated," he says at last to me.

"No I didn't!" I protest.

"He didn't, sir," Electra adds.

"Cheating and insubordination," Monitor Gorget snaps. He points at my inside-out jacket. "And out of uniform." He turns to Electra. "For failure to maintain your squad in good order, Squad Leader, you get four faults and a night on the punishment parade."

He points at me. "And as for you," he says, his voice rasping with disapproval, "your punishment is more severe. You, Cadet Trouble, are about to go join the rats in the quiet room."

Sekka gives a prim nod, approving of my punishment, but Drigo and Rose exchange a wide-eyed worried glance, and even Tyran looks a little sick.

As Gorget scowls down at me, I pretend to be sad and chastened, but I'm not here to be a good cadet; I'm here to help rescue Miracle Zox, so what I'm really thinking is *Finally!*

35

The quiet room is exactly as Drigo described
it. It's a small, cold box of a room dug out of the stone deep
under the academy. It's barely big enough to stand up in. Icy
dampness seeps from the walls, and the air smells like cold
stone and rot. It's completely dark and empty except for a
drain in the floor.

It's *perfect*.

Without a word, Monitor Gorget takes my warm jacket
and my boots and socks and shoves me into the quiet room,
then slams the door, and I hear the sound of metal clicking
and clunking, which I assume is a lock.

Good. I bet he's going to leave me in here for at least a day.
This gives me plenty of time to do what I came here to do,
which is get to Electra's sister and start our escape.

But first I have to talk to Electra, who, fortunately for me, but not for her, is on punishment parade.

I shift into my rat form, leaving my Cadet Trouble ID chip on the floor in the quiet room, and slither into the drain. It's slimy and dark, but rats have left clear scent marks, so I have no trouble at all finding my way through a maze of pipes and heating ducts until I come out inside the Stores room.

That's where I was given my uniform and other kit, remember?

It's after dinner now, so the Stores room is deserted. I shift back into my human boy form and rummage through the shelves until I find a pair of socks, which I eat while finding a coverall that fits me and some more socks, which I put on, and a warm blanket to take with me. Keeping my ears pricked, I go out the Stores door and into a dark corridor. It must be later than I thought, because there's nobody around.

On my quiet sock feet I pad through the corridors to the entrance hall, and I barely crack the main doors and slide outside. The sky is clouded over and snow is sifting down. I cross the cold stones to Electra, who is standing in the middle of the courtyard. At attention, of course.

"Hello," I say as I come up to her.

"T," she says.

I found this out during my punishment parade last night— when you're very cold, your teeth rattle together. And that's not even the weirdest thing about teeth. I mean, if you think about it, teeth are, what, *bones*? That stick out of your body!

And human teeth—so strangely flat, not very sharp or bitey, really.

Anyway, Electra's teeth are clenched together so they don't rattle.

I sling the blanket over her shoulders and then move closer to share my warmth with her. "All right," I say. "Tell me what's going on."

"I d-d-don't know if you're a genius, T, or the biggest idiot on this entire planet," she says, shivering.

"Possibly both," I admit.

She snorts. "You'd better not stay long, just in case Gorget looks out a window." She steps closer to me and raises her arm, sharing the blanket, and we huddle together. "All right. You know about my sister, and if you can get to her tonight, do it. Can you find your way there?"

"Yep," I answer.

"Good," Electra says. "Tell her to be ready for an escape."

"When?" I ask.

"Soon," she says. "The monitors have a ship on the tower landing pad."

My human heart gives a little jolt of excitement. "Are we going to steal it?"

"No," she answers. "Borrow. We'll use it to get to Dreadknot, and our mother's ship will pick us up and take us to safety, where the StarLeague can't track our ID chips."

"Well . . ." I say slowly.

She makes a sound like *arrrgggghhhhh*. "I *knew* you'd make this difficult. What, T. What do you want to do differently?"

"What about Drigo?" I ask. "He has nightmares, did you know that? And I bet Rose would like to get away too, and there must be others who were stolen from their families and want to go home."

"I'm sure there are," Electra says with a sigh. "But we can't load them all onto a shuttle and escape."

"We have to think of something," I tell her. Suddenly I feel a fierce, deep longing to see my mom. I *miss* her terribly. "I wish Captain Astra were here. She'd know what to do."

Electra gives me a hug. "She would. We'll do the best we can, all right?"

I nod because misery water—tears—of missing my mom have spilled out of my eyes and onto my face. I wipe them off with a corner of the blanket. "What about the other thing?" I mumble.

I feel Electra stiffen. "Yes," she says sharply. "Something big is happening. Our training has been accelerated, and I think a lot of the most elite cadets, including our squad, are about to be sent on a mission."

"That's not usual?" I ask.

"The only other time it happened, they needed us to help pursue a certain shapeshifter who had escaped from a level-four military weapons lab facility."

"Hah," I say, because she's talking about me. "What's the new mission?"

"We don't know," Electra says. "But I have a feeling it's

something very dangerous and it's happening very soon. The monitors and other officers are on edge."

When she says this, I remember the two soldiers I overheard on the troop transport ship. "There *is* something," I say. "A threat of some kind at the edge of the galaxy. Lots of soldiers are being called up."

Electra nods. "Maybe that's it. I don't know."

I glance up at the night sky, but it's covered with clouds, so I can't see if the stars that blinked out the other night are still missing. Do they have something to do with this too?

"We have to get my sister, Miracle," Electra goes on, "and get out of here before this mission begins. Got it?"

Got it.

Taking the blanket with me, I leave Electra to her snow parade, and I head back into the academy building to follow a rat scent trail to find Miracle Zox.

36

You might be wondering why I don't just shift into my Hunter form, grab Electra and her sister, steal the shuttle, and blast out of the academy.

A bunch of reasons.

One, it's an academy full of highly trained soldiers who are also kids like me. I don't want to scare them, and I also don't want anybody to get hurt.

Two, if the people in charge of the academy find out there are two shapeshifters here, they'll start tracking the special shifting energy, and they'll try to trap me and Donut down here on the planet.

Three, I really don't want to escape without sad-eyed Drigo and Rose and all the other cadets who don't want to be here, especially the ones who were stolen from their families.

Four, Electra can pilot a Dart, which is small; flying a ship big enough to fit everybody is way more complicated, and I'm not sure she can do it.

Five, I don't want to give the StarLeague another reason to come after me.

And then there's reason number six.

Because I am either a genius or the stupidest person on the planet, one or the other, I sneak into Miracle's squad's bunk room as a rat and do *not* shift into my human-boy Trouble shape, but into a mantis form, like the perfect cadet Sekka.

Being in an insectoid shape is hard to adjust to after being in my usual human form. For humans, everything is *so* bright and colorful and loud, and food tastes delicious, and human emotions swirl with adrenaline and hormones, and are deeply confusing most of the time. Insectoids are very similar to each other and have an intense bond with others in their clans, but other species are sort of . . . distant to them. Their senses are not keen, and their carapaces—outer skeletons, like armor—mean they're protected all the time. They're kind of the opposite of squishy, exposed, emotional humans.

Anyway, I shift into the mantis form and go quietly to Miracle Zox's bunk. She is asleep, and her tintacles are wrapped up, but I can see that she looks strong and determined like Electra, but younger. I poke her with one of my antennae.

After I dodge her attack and hold her hands with my fore-legs, I lean close and hiss, *Shhhhhhhhhh*.

"Who are you?" she gasps.

"A friend," I whisper.

"Why shouldn't I call out my squad to capture you and turn you in to the monitors?" she whispers back.

"Because," I tell her, "your sister, Electra, sent me. She is here."

Then she really surprises me.

"I know," she says. "So what?"

Because I'm not completely stupid, I don't tell her that Electra has come back to the academy to rescue her.

"Do you want to escape from here?" I ask in my clicky mantis voice. "And go back to your family?"

"Why would I?" she whispers back. "My family sent me here when I was a tiny baby; why should I want to go back to them?"

Before I can explain to her that she was kidnapped by the StarLeague, Miracle goes on.

"Anyway, I have a squad to take care of. And we're needed."

"Needed?" I repeat. "For what?"

Miracle Zox sits up and wraps her arms around her knees, then leans closer to speak. "The senior cadet squads will be called up soon. There's some sort of threat coming from the Deep Dark."

Mantises don't nod, but I twitch an antenna at her. "Tell me more," I say.

"Why should I?" Miracle Zox challenges.

"I'm very curious," I answer.

She gives me a suspicious look. "I've never met a curious mantis before. What did you say your name was?"

Oop. "It's Trouble," I say, because lying tastes so terrible. "Just tell me about the threat from the Deep Dark."

She shrugs. "All right. Two trading ships have disappeared, and the StarLeague military ship that was sent to investigate also disappeared. *Then* an asteroid was taken. One of my cadets says he heard that a planet is in danger—it might be next."

"Disappeared?" I repeat, remembering the stars that blinked out when I was in the courtyard on my punishment parade.

Miracle nods. "That's what I said."

"But what's making things disappear?" I ask, feeling strangely nervous all of a sudden. "I mean, a *planet*?" *Stars??*

"*I* don't know," Miracle says irritably. "It's not my job to know. It's like they're being eaten; that's what we've heard. It's some kind of weapon, maybe? An enemy from another galaxy? It doesn't matter. My cadet squad is the best of all the juniors, and we want to be part of the fight. Now"—she points at the door—"go away, strange mantis cadet named Trouble."

"But," I protest in my clicky voice, "you weren't sent away by your family. You have a mother and a sister who want you back."

"Oh *really*," Miracle scoffs. "I've been here for ten years.

What's taking them so long? Now get *out*. Before I raise the alarm."

I scuttle out.

So that's reason number six. The miraculous Miracle Zox doesn't want to be rescued.

And she maybe has a very good reason for wanting to stay.

On my way back to the quiet room, I stop off at Stores to eat some more socks and a pair of boots, but I'm distracted, trying to figure out what we're going to do about Electra's sister.

Because I *know* for *certain* that both Electra and I believe that kids like us get to choose for ourselves what we want to do. So we can't exactly force Miracle Zox to leave if she wants to stay, even if the academy is awful.

And then there's the problem of the big mission that both Electra and Miracle think is coming up. Something in the Deep Dark that can destroy an entire planet? I remember that the blackdragon and the nebula crabs were fleeing something from the Deep Dark, and I remember the creepy feeling of being watched when we were at the *Skeleton*, and the disappearing stars, and I think there really *is* something out there, something terrible and dangerous, something that could eat an entire planet, an entire star. What if Miracle Zox is sent on the mission to deal with it? What if she's hurt, or even killed? Does that mean we should decide for her?

I don't know what to do.

For now, all I can do is shift into a rat and go back through the maze of pipes and into the quiet room, where I shift back into my human boy shape—making sure to shift around the ID chip—and put on my uniform.

I sit on the stone floor of the cold, damp, dark quiet room and wrap my arms around my knees and start to shiver. I could shift into a shape that doesn't mind the cold, but I'd rather be in my human boy shape.

And then, in the dark, something soft bumps against my leg.

A rat?

I reach out with my hand and my fingers brush against a . . . fringed edge? It's not rat fur. My fingers feel stiff, bumpy cloth.

It's a stripy pillow with fringes around the edges. Oh, and it's added fluffy pom-poms at each corner.

"Hello, Donut," I say to it. My voice is swallowed up by the darkness, so it sounds small and a little lost.

Under my fingers, the bumpy cloth changes, growing softer and spreading wide, until I realize that Donut has shifted itself into a warm, fluffy blanket.

"Is it all right if I wrap myself up in you?" I ask.

The blanket nudges my leg, which I guess means yes, so I get up and wrap the Donut-blanket around me and sit down in a corner. Donut is warmer than a real blanket, and I sit there in the dark feeling cozy and safe and sleepy.

Waaaaaait a minute.

I blink, suddenly wide awake because I've just realized something, and it makes me feel awful.

A donut.

A sock.

A highly decorated pillow.

A blaster.

A pile of protein bars.

A mug that said **GaLIXYS beST CATPiAN** on it.

All those are things Donut has shifted into, and they are all things that my family on the *Hindsight* like. And now a blanket to keep me warm. All this time, I realize, Donut wasn't being obnoxious; it was trying to be useful. Maybe it even wants us to like it.

"I'm sorry, Donut," I whisper. Carefully, I pull a corner of the blanket to my face and give it a kiss, just like my mom kisses the top of my head when she gives me a hug. It's like what she said—families are complicated. "I'll try to be a better big sibling to you," I tell it.

The blanket snuggles up to me. I hope that means it's all right.

Feeling better, I settle in to do some thinking, because there's a lot going on.

I think about what the StarLeague's upcoming big, dangerous mission might be, and the fact that their last big, dangerous mission was to recapture me. And I think about Reetha's cryptic words to me about the suspicious signal from the *Skeleton*, and why the *Hindsight* just happened to be the ship that received that signal. And I think about the black-dragon and the nebula crabs and nightmares and weapons labs and stars blinking out of existence. And I remember that the two soldiers on the troop transport ship said something about the Deep Dark. And I think about patient Commander Io and her warning about shapeshifter bombs.

And I wonder if all of those things have something to do with each other.

Something to do with *me*.

37

The lock in the door goes *clank, clunk*. As I get stiffly to my feet, Donut helpfully shifts from its cozy, warm blanket form into the shape of a small stone. I close my hand over it and slip it into the pocket of my coverall just before the door swings open.

After being in the dark for so long, even the dim light of the underground corridor is too bright, and I shield my eyes, blinking. "Hello!" I say.

Monitor Gorget looks me up and down. "Sounds like you need some more time in the quiet room."

"It doesn't matter how long you leave me in here," I tell him. "It's not going to make a difference. I'm not good at sameyness."

"*Sameyness?*" he asks, giving me a narrow-eyed, suspicious look.

"I can't even be the same as myself," I say. "There's no way I can be the same as everybody else."

"Try harder," he says grimly, and hands me my socks and boots.

I sit on the stone floor to put them on. "Monitor Gorget," I ask, because I had plenty of time to think about the questions I need answered, "is there a big mission coming up?"

With a bony hand, he reaches down and grabs me by the front of my coverall, dragging me to my feet. "What have you heard about it, Cadet?"

"Not much," I say. "I'm just wondering about the tactics. If the cadets are being sent into danger."

"That's what you're *for*, Cadet," he rasps. "Or had you forgotten?"

"I'm not sure *what* I'm for," I tell him—truthfully, as it happens.

He lets me go, pushing me away as if he's disgusted with me. "Your job is to obey orders."

I finish putting on my boots, and then he leads me along the corridor and up narrow stairs cut out of the rock, until we go through a door at the top and out into the world.

It's night again, so once Gorget dismisses me, I head for Double-star Squad's bunk room. On the way I stop at the Stores room, shift into my blob of goo form and eat a bunch of clothes and boots and things, shift back into my human boy shape and get dressed again, and hurry to the Double-star Squad room. I need to talk to Electra, and I can't wait to get her alone.

I creep into the bunk room. It's dark and quiet—everybody is asleep. The Donut stone is still in my pocket, so I take it out and leave it on my neatly made bed, and then go to Electra's bunk.

She's awake. "Are you all right, T?" she whispers.

What a question. "Of course I am," I whisper back. "I talked to Miracle."

Electra is just a shadow in the darker night, but I can see her lean forward. "And?"

"She doesn't want to leave," I whisper. "And she thinks your mother gave her to the StarLeague."

"What!?" Electra hisses through her teeth.

And I realize that we're being spied on. I can see two greenish points of light in the bunk above mine. "Your eyes glow in the dark, Tyran," I say aloud.

The lights blink out.

"You'd better come down here," I tell him.

There's a slither and a quiet thump, and Tyran comes over and crouches next to Electra's bed, his eyes glowing green. We make a small circle there in the dark. "I *knew* you were up to something," he whispers.

"What are you going to do about it?" I ask him. "We know you've been spying on Double-star Squad and reporting to Monitor Gorget."

"What?" he squeaks. The lights of his eyes flicker—he's blinking rapidly.

"Every squad has a spy in it, Tyran," Electra says quietly. "We know it's you."

"It's *not* me," Tyran protests. "Just because I don't *like* you doesn't mean I'm *spying* on you."

There's another rustle and the pad of footsteps, and big, quiet Rose pushes his way into our group. "What's going on?" he whispers.

"A very good question," Tyran answers. "They haven't said anything useful yet."

"Shhhhh," Electra says.

"But we all *know* you've been acting very suspiciously," Tyran goes on.

Another dark shadow leans down from the top bunk across from us. "I'm awake," it whispers. Drigo. "And I know you're up to something too."

Electra sighs. "You might as well turn on the light."

Drigo climbs out of his bed and goes to the door, where he taps a button; overhead the light flickers on. From the top bunk over our heads, the mantis cadet, Sekka, sticks her head out, antennae twitching. Always watching, Sekka. But she doesn't climb down.

Drigo sits on the floor with both of his puppy ears cocked, alert; Rose crouches next to him. Electra and I sit on the bed, and Tyran stands with arms crossed, his forked tongue flicking out to test the air. I'm about to ask him why we should believe him when he says he's not the spy, when he asks a question of his own.

"All right, tell us. What *are* you?" Tyran asks, pointing at me.

"I'm a cadet just like you," I answer.

Rose folds his brawny arms and shakes his head. Even Drigo looks like he doesn't believe me. "How stupid do you think we are?" Tyran spits out.

"Don't answer that question, Trouble," Electra interrupts before I can say anything. She nods at me. "Tell them."

Even better, I'll show them. I get to my feet and shift into my dog puppy shape. Not too scary, right? But it makes Drigo gasp and scuttle backward across the floor, while Rose leaps to his feet and Tyran scrambles away. And from the top bunk, Sekka jumps to the floor and darts toward the door.

"Grab her!" Electra shouts.

In a flash, I shift into the Hunter form and blur to the door, getting there before Sekka can wrench it open.

"She's the spy," Tyran gasps.

What? Perfect cadet Sekka? No!

Sekka immediately proves that she *is* the spy because she pulls a blaster out of her coverall pocket and shoots at me. Big mistake! The Hunter deflects the blaster bolt, picks up Sekka—careful not to hurt her—and takes her to the bathroom, shoving her inside as she struggles and flails. I close the door and drip my fang-poison on the lock so she can't open it again. Then I turn to face the cadets.

Drigo, Rose, and Tyran are all staring at me—at the Hunter's fearsome fangs and shoulder spikes and impenetrable armor. I wave a claw at them. *See? Still me.*

"Wow," Drigo says, which is what you say when you're really surprised by something.

"Yeah," Rose says.

"That," Tyran adds, "was *not* what I expected."

38

After I've shifted back into my human boy shape and put my coverall on again, I sit next to Electra on her bunk.

"You're a shapeshifter," Drigo says, staring at me. His puppy nose twitches.

"Yep," I answer.

Tyran's black eyes narrow suspiciously. "Waaaaait. He's *the* shapeshifter. The one we were sent to recapture during our first mission."

"That's right," I tell him. A stripy, fringey, pom-pommed pillow has appeared on Electra's bed, but I'm not going to explain about Donut. One shapeshifter is hard enough for them to deal with.

"And you were *not* kidnapped," Tyran accuses Electra. "You and the shapeshifter were friends all along!"

But Electra's not paying him any attention. She's staring blankly ahead. "Our first mission," she repeats. "Wait a minute."

Suddenly I feel a little shivery. She's thinking the same thoughts I had while I was in the quiet room. She's adding some things up.

"I just realized something," Electra says.

"What?" I ask.

She shifts her gaze and looks intently at me. "How old are you?"

"No idea," I tell her. "I can't remember that far back."

"If you really were a human boy, you'd be about . . ." She nods. "About twelve years old, as humans calculate age." She points to herself. "I was taken by the StarLeague twelve years ago."

"So was I," Tyran puts in.

"You *were*?" I ask, trying to remember if there was a skinny, annoying lizardian—one of Tyran's parents—among Min Zox's fighters.

"Shut up," Tyran hisses at me.

"Yes, shut up, T, so I can think," Electra says. "Twelve years ago is when the StarLeague started their cadet training program." Her eyes grow wide. "And the *Skeleton* was lost for how long?" she asks.

"Twelve years," I say, even though she already knows the answer.

"Twelve," she repeats.

"What are you talking about?" Tyran interrupts.

We both ignore him.

"Twelve years ago," Electra says slowly, "the StarLeague started training cadets for special missions. And they created a shapeshifter—a Hunter. Why?" She stands up and starts pacing. "Why did the StarLeague stop exploring and helping people and start building military ships like the *Peacemaker*? Why do they need a Hunter and cadets like us?"

"To use as weapons—" I say.

She interrupts. "Against who?" She frowns. "Or *what*? What have they been preparing for for twelve years? Is that the big mission that's coming up?"

It's time to tell her and the others what Electra's sister told me. "Miracle Zox told me that two trading ships and a StarLeague ship and an asteroid have all disappeared. They think a planet might be next. And when I was on my punishment parade I saw two stars disappear."

"Stars don't just disappear," Tyran scoffs.

"Miracle said," I go on, "that maybe it's a new weapon, or an enemy from another galaxy. And, Electra, remember the blackdragon and the nebula crabs, how afraid they were of something in the Deep Dark? And the missing crew of the *Skeleton*?"

Electra nods. "Yes."

"Miracle said . . ." I take a deep breath. "She said that it's like the ships and the asteroid were eaten, and I think that's what the blackdragon was afraid of too. Of being eaten."

Electra's gaze sharpens. "Eaten?" she asks.

I nod.

She gazes at me for a stretched-out second. Then she frowns and shakes her head. "Here's what I think. Twelve years ago the StarLeague found out about this disappearing or eating or whatever. An Eater. Very dangerous, whatever it is. That's when the StarLeague made you, Trouble, and they made the cadets to fight it."

"So I'm sort of like a cadet," I put in. "Made to fight the Eater from the Deep Dark. Just like you."

"You," Tyran says with a snort, "are *nothing* like us."

"Shut up," Electra snaps. "Stay focused. It's clear that the Eater is not waiting around out there in the Deep Dark. It's about to invade our galaxy."

"Or maybe," I say slowly, "it's already here."

"It must be," Rose puts in, surprisingly. "Because at dinner last night I heard a rumor." His pink eyes flicker from one of us to the next, around the circle. Then he nods. "I heard our mission starts tomorrow."

"So," I ask. "What next?"

Electra sits down on the bed next to me. Her face has turned sharp and determined. "Strategy," she says slowly, as if she's thinking something over. Then she nods. "Tomorrow the StarLeague is going to send the cadets to fight this thing.

The Eater. Their tactics involve us getting killed—or eaten, whatever. We're not going to let that happen."

"What're we going to do?" Tyran asks.

Electra looks at him. *"We?"*

"We," says Drigo, his furry face serious.

"Yes, we," Rose adds.

I feel a flicker of happiness and hope. Our squad is becoming a team, almost like a little family.

"I think I should tell you," I say to them, "that Electra and I met your parents."

Rose's pink face goes even pinker. "You met my dad?" he blurts out.

Drigo takes a gasping breath, and his sad eyes fill with tears.

"They miss you and want you back," I tell them. "If you want to go back to them."

"We all do," Tyran puts in.

"I think . . . well . . ." I glance over at Electra, and because she's my best friend, she knows what I'm thinking. She nods. "I think that if you want to go home now, we can help you do that. You don't have to be cadets, and you don't have to fight the Eater, whatever it is."

"You're saying we get to choose," Tyran says slowly.

"Yep," I reply, and I repeat what my mom said to me about choosing. "Always."

The three of them—Rose, Tyran, and Drigo—share a look. Drigo blinks, Rose raises his eyebrows, and then all three nod. "We'll help you deal with the Eater," Tyran answers for all of them. "We're a squad." He gives me a nice sort of sneer. "Including you, Cadet Shapeshifter."

"Thanks." I turn to Electra. "And your sister, Miracle, should be on the team too. She's fierce, and we'll need her, and I think she'll want to come."

"Yes," Electra agrees. "All right."

It's funny. I'm the most powerful being in the galaxy, right? Or maybe I'm not, depending on what this Eater actually is. But it's *Electra* who is the leader of our team, not me. She's the one who knows strategy and tactics; she's the one who is in charge.

"Here's the plan," Electra says, leaning forward.

The rest of us lean in too, to hear what she wants us to do.

39

The first thing we have to do, Electra says, is get ourselves off this planet so we can't be used as weapons by the StarLeague. We can't wait until tomorrow night because of Sekka the Spy locked in the bathroom and also because the cadets' mission is supposed to start soon. We have to do it now. Then we'll figure out what comes next. We'll seek out the Eater and fight it on our own terms, with *our* strategy. And if we survive that, we'll make sure *all* the cadets get to go home to their families.

It's almost morning and the cadets in the huge stone academy building will be waking up soon. If I hurry, Electra says, I can get to Miracle Zox and join the rest of the squad at the meeting point without anybody catching us.

In my human boy shape I race through the corridors, stopping now and then to shift into my rat form so I can sniff my way toward Miracle's squad's room.

When I get there, I don't bother knocking, I just barge in. Miracle Zox sits straight up in bed, her tintacles escaping from their wrappings, and stares at me.

"Hello!" I say, strangely glad to see her.

"Who are *you*?" she demands, climbing out of her bunk.

Oop. I wasn't in this shape when I met her before. "I'm the mantis," I tell her. "Trouble. I talked to you the other night, remember?"

Her eyes narrow suspiciously. Reaching under her pillow, she pulls out a knife. The other cadets are peering over the edges of their bunks; one of them, a lizardian, has started climbing down to the floor.

Yeeks. I don't want to fight them.

"I'm a shapeshifter," I say to Miracle. "I'm your sister Electra's best friend."

Miracle Zox steps closer to me, keeping her knife at the ready. "You're *the* shapeshifter? The escaped criminal shapeshifter that the senior cadets were sent to capture not that long ago?"

"Yep!" I say. "That's me, except I'm not a criminal, I'm a kid. And I'm in a hurry. I need you to come with me."

"Hah," she says, sounding a lot like Electra. "Not a chance." She makes some signal to the others in her squad, and they all leap out of their bunks. "Get him!"

All six of the cadets jump on me and I *don't* shift out of my human boy shape, so they pin me to the floor, holding my arms and legs. Miracle Zox puts the knife to my neck.

"I really don't have time for this," I gasp, trying to wriggle away.

"Shut up," growls the lizardian, who is sprawled across my chest, holding me down.

"Go fetch the monitor," Miracle orders, and one of the cadets lets go of my arm and heads for the door.

Rats. Electra told me to sneak in, get Miracle, and sneak out without anybody catching us. Quiet! Stealthy! No alarms!

Oh well.

"Watch out," I warn, and then I shift into my Hunter shape.

Ignoring their yells and shrugging off their attacks with my incredible speed and impenetrable armor, I grab my coverall, pick up Miracle Zox, and zip out of the room and race down the hallway so fast that I'm around the corner before the cadets even reach the door.

Miracle is all stabbity-stab with her knife, but it doesn't bother the Hunter. I try carrying her so she doesn't get stuck on my razor-sharp spikes and wish she would quit yelling so loudly.

I know, I know. I'm not supposed to be kidnapping Miracle; I'm supposed to let her choose. But she needs to see Electra first. *Then* she can decide.

As I zoom along—weirdly, the Hunter can sense exactly which way to go—the academy starts to stir. An alarm goes off in the distance, a siren that starts low and builds to a shrill shriek that echoes through the hallways. Cadets start spilling out of their rooms. I'm moving so fast that they barely have time to react before I've already blurred past them.

Excuse me! Coming through!

Finally I burst out the main doors into the courtyard—still carrying Miracle, who is *still* struggling mightily—and lope across the stones to the meeting place, which is the middle of the courtyard where the punishment parade happens. Electra is there, holding the Donut-pillow, along with Drigo, Rose, and a nervous-looking Tyran.

Carefully, I set Miracle down, and gently take the knife out of her hands.

Electra and her sister face each other. It's the first time they've ever met.

I'm pretty sure there's not going to be any hugging.

"There's a threat approaching from the Deep Dark," Electra snaps out. "We're going to deal with it. Want to join us?"

Miracle Zox catches her breath. "Why now? Why not just wait until later when the StarLeague mission begins?"

Oh, so she's heard the rumor too.

"We're doing this on *our* terms," Electra explains. "And you don't have to go on any mission at all; you can come with us and we can make sure you're safe."

Miracle nods at me. "Is this weird shapeshifter-boy-monster-thing friend of yours coming?"

"That's Trouble," Electra says sharply. "And yes."

"It says it's your best friend," Miracle says.

For some reason being near Miracle makes me want to show off, so I shift from my Hunter shape to storker to puppy. I bark at her. *Aroo!*

She's staring. "That is the strangest thing I have ever seen."

I shift back into my Hunter form. *Yes, Miracle. I am deeply weird. But are you coming with us?*

She stares at me for another second and then shrugs. "Well, this could be interesting." She gives Electra a snappy salute. "I'm in, Squad Leader."

Electra blinks. "I'm . . . I'm not your squad leader. I'm your sister." She glances over at me, but I'm in my Hunter form, so I can't exactly tell her what to do.

But she's seen me and the captain when we've been apart for a long time. "Um," Electra says slowly. "I think we should probably hug."

"Really?" Miracle says dubiously.

Electra frowns, then nods. "Yes. That is what family does. We should, if you want to."

There in the courtyard, with the alarms going off all around, Electra and Miracle step closer. Electra turns and hands me Donut to hold in my claws, and then she opens her arms. Frowning, Miracle opens hers, and awkwardly, as if they're both all bony elbows and stiff backs, they hug.

"I'm glad that's over with," Miracle says, stepping away. "Now what, Sister Squad Leader?"

Electra straightens and points at the tall tower in the middle of the academy building. "The monitors' shuttle is parked on the landing pad up there." She gives us a sudden, wide grin. "Let's go steal it."

40

Compared to kidnapping Miracle Zox, steal-ing the academy shuttle is easy.

As alarms go off and monitors run through the halls shouting orders, I shift back into my human boy shape and drag on my coverall, and then we race across the stone courtyard to the main doors of the academy—seven of us counting Donut, who Electra is carrying.

We step in the door and come face-to-face with Monitor Gorget and his metal club. "Hold it right there," he orders.

"They went that way!" Electra shouts, and points at the open door leading to the courtyard. "If you hurry, you can catch them!"

Monitor Gorget doesn't even hesitate.

As he disappears through the main door, Miracle says, "Huh. That was easy."

"Come on!" Electra shouts, leading us to the stairs that wind up to the very top of the main tower.

"It's going to get a lot harder," I say, following Miracle up the stairs.

"Yes, I know," she pants, and glances over her shoulder at me. "I *am* a cadet, unlike you."

Puffing and panting, we climb up until we reach the landing pad, where, sure enough, there's a shuttle.

"Get aboard!" Electra orders, and the rest of us squeeze inside while she slides into the pilot's seat, carefully setting down the Donut-pillow next to her.

A quick glance over her shoulder shows her that the shuttle is barely big enough to hold all of us. "Trouble!" she orders, and I know what she wants me to do, so I shift into my rat form—"Ew!" Miracle Zox protests—to give everybody else more room.

Then a bright blue bolt of blaster fire splashes across the nose of the shuttle. It's followed by a loud, rattling boom; Rose loses his balance and almost steps on me in my rat form. *Careful!*

Tyran—surprisingly—stoops and picks me up, setting me on his shoulder and then wedging himself more tightly into a corner.

"Hang on," Electra says, pushing buttons on the control panel. The shuttle door slams closed.

A moment later, the shuttle lurches upward and then banks sharply, and the four cadets—and me!—are squished against the opposite wall in a tangle of arms and legs and one rat tail.

"Get *off* me," Miracle protests, shoving Rose's elbow out of her face.

"Ow," Drigo says in a muffled voice.

Electra slams her hand on another button and pushes a lever forward, and the shuttle lurches again and I catch a glimpse of another, bigger laser blast zipping past the front window, and then we start to climb steeply, until the cadets and I are pasted against the back wall of the shuttle.

In the pilot's seat, Electra is leaning forward, her teeth gritted, pushing buttons, muttering, "Come on, *come on*," and the shuttle shakes and bumps for more long minutes, and then, suddenly, we pop out of the planet's atmosphere.

We don't even have time to catch our breaths or get untangled from each other.

"*Rats*," Electra curses.

Speaking of rats, I jump off of Tyran's shoulder and scamper to the pilot's seat, where I run up Electra's leg and onto the control panel. From there I can see out the shuttle's front window.

And of course. Of *course*.

There, hanging sleek and silver against the deep blue-black of space, is the StarLeague *Arrow*.

41

"That's the *Arrow*," Electra says, staring at the ship that is looming large through the shuttle's front window. "Commander Io. What is she doing here?"

"Who's Commander Io?" Tyran demands. He's wedged next to bulky Rose and Drigo and Miracle, with Electra in the pilot's seat.

I'm sitting in my rat form on the shuttle's control panel. Electra gives me a sharp look. "She didn't just get here, did she?" She frowns. "She's been waiting."

Fortunately, I'm currently a rat, so I don't have to answer any questions about Commander Io.

She called me a shapeshifter bomb, remember? I know that Electra needs to know about that, even though she's going to be mad I didn't tell her before that I went to talk to Commander Io, and . . . and . . .

. . . I have a terrible feeling about what's really going on, and I have to think about what it means that the *Arrow* has been here all along, waiting for me.

I hope my mom and the *Hindsight* are around here somewhere too.

Electra reaches down and pulls my coverall from the floor under Drigo's feet. "Shift, Trouble," she orders, and holds it up.

I stay in my rat form.

The *Arrow* grows larger; it's pulling us into an open docking bay.

My stomach growls loudly, so loudly that all the cadets stare at me, eyes wide.

"Give him some room," Electra says, and the other cadets squish themselves toward the back of the shuttle.

Nope. Not shifting.

My stomach growls loudly again. I've done a lot of shifting, and I haven't had enough to eat, and no actual food for a long time. Hours. *Days.*

"*Trouble*," Electra snaps. "We're about to be captured by a StarLeague commander who has been incredibly persistent in following you. I need some information! Why is Commander Io here? Does she have something to do with the StarLeague's mission to fight the Eater? What do you know?"

"I thought you said you were friends," Miracle puts in.

"We *are*," Electra says impatiently. "He's just being stubborn."

I'm being a rat, is what.

"*Trouble*," Electra protests.

There's a loud *clunk* and a *thunk*, and our shuttle sets down in the *Arrow*'s docking bay. The door to the shuttle unseals and slides open. Outside, in the large airlock, StarLeague soldiers in black uniforms are waiting. They're all carrying heavy blaster guns.

"Gah!" Electra exclaims. She leans down to speak to me. "T, they know that the Hunter could take their ship apart without even trying."

"It *could*?" Miracle interrupts.

"You've seen the Hunter," Electra says. "It's incredibly powerful. The StarLeague is terrified of it." She scowls down at me. "T, they know they can't recapture you. *What* is going on?!"

And then the soldiers are at the door of the shuttle pointing guns at the cadets. With his hands up, Drigo edges out, followed by Rose, Tyran, and then Miracle Zox, who shoots me a glare as she steps off the shuttle.

Electra huffs out a sigh, leaves Donut, which isn't like her, and goes out.

A moment later I skitter out on my little rat-feet, unnoticed, and head for the nearest hiding place, a shadowy corner where I can see what's happening.

The five cadets are lined up at attention, all except for Miracle Zox, who is scowling in my general direction. I twitch my whiskers at her, but she's probably too far away to see.

"Commander on the dock!" one of the StarLeague soldiers announces, and now they're *all* standing at attention while Commander Io strides through the main door. She glances at the shuttle parked there, taking up most of the space, and then surveys the five cadets.

She stops in front of Electra. "Cadet, we've been monitoring the unique energy signal the shapeshifter emits when it shifts. We know it was on the shuttle with you."

Electra continues to stare straight ahead and doesn't even blink. "What shapeshifter?"

Miracle Zox opens her mouth as if she's about to say something; then she glances at Electra and stays quiet.

Commander Io studies her for a long moment, a patient look on her brown, wrinkly face. "Does anyone else wish to comment?" she asks.

If I know Tyran, he'll have a comment—and not a good one.

"No, ma'am!" Tyran raps out, and a moment later Drigo, Rose, and Miracle echo, *No, ma'am.*

Wow. Maybe we really are *a squad!*

"I see," Commander Io says. She turns to one of the soldiers. "These cadets are to be given a bunk room together and something to eat. Be sure that they are continuously monitored. They are to be very well treated during their time on my ship. Understood?"

The soldier nods, and the other soldiers lower their guns.

"Go with them, Cadets," Commander Io orders.

After a moment, Electra gives a sharp nod, and the five cadets march out after the soldiers.

Commander Io turns to follow them out, but then she pauses in the doorway. "Trouble," she says loudly, her voice echoing in the high-ceilinged docking bay, "I know that you are here. I am setting a course for the edge of the galaxy, not far from the *Skeleton*. An entire star system with four inhabited planets and two inhabited moons is in immediate danger. Billions of people could be lost. And that's just the beginning—the entire galaxy is under threat. I need to speak with you as soon as possible."

42

Do you remember what Commander Io told me before? Not the part about the *shapeshifter bomb,* but the other thing.

She told me that my *actual purpose* was to be a weapon, but not in the way I expected.

She told me that I have something to do with the *fate of the entire galaxy.*

And I scoffed at that!

But now I think Commander Io knows all about me and what I am and what I'm for, and I think she really was there in that nightmare military weapons lab. I suspect she may not be as kind as she looks. I think she knew all along that Electra was not kidnapped, but my friend, and she let her go to Apex-9 because she knew I would follow.

I'm not sure I can trust her.

Rats.

I know who I *can* trust. Electra. And our squad.

Before I go find them, I have to eat. Still in my rat form, I follow a scent trail from the docking bay through some pipes into the ship's galley. It's all shiny, clean metal, and it's much bigger than the cozy, homey kitchen on the *Hindsight*. For a second I miss home so much, it's worse than hunger. I wonder where Captain Astra—my mom—is right now. Is she worried about me? I'm worried about her, anyway.

The *Arrow*'s galley is empty and dark, so I shift into my human boy form—I'm not giving myself away, Io already knows I'm here—and find some actual humanoid food. Sitting on the shiny, spotlessly clean galley floor, I eat a huge pot of stew that was left on a counter. Mmmm, stew, I have missed you so much! My stomach is still rumbling hungrily, so I also eat twenty-five protein bars and an entire cake that I find on a cooling rack, and some lizardian salt snacks, and five blocks of tofu, and a pot of spicy rice.

I burp. Oop. I think I just ate the entire *Arrow* crew's entire dinner.

Strangely, I'm still a little hungry, but I'm all right for now.

I shift back into my rat form and head for the pipes. It isn't long before I meet up with some of the *Arrow*'s rats. There in the narrow metal pipe, I touch noses with a gray-pelted female who understands that I'm an honorary rat. The rats on this ship probably know more about what's really going on than Commander Io does, but they won't get involved unless they absolutely have to. They want people to keep thinking that they're just rats and not galactic genius masterminds.

Leaving the rat, I follow scent marks through the ship until I come to a ventilation tube high in the wall of the room where the cadets are being held prisoner. Interestingly, the grate that covers it has already been removed. I peek out.

All five of the cadets are there. The room has six bunk beds in it, and a few comfortable chairs and a table that has the remains of their lunch on it. A screen takes up one entire wall. There's a stripy pillow on one of the bunks. I wonder how Donut got here before I did.

The cadets are staring intently at the screen, watching a news broadcast from The Knowledge. Even in my rat form, The Knowledge's deep voice gives me the shivers.

—in the outer rim colony. Evacuation of inhabitants of the Xyrch system has begun. Military weapons scientists from the StarLeague still do not know the nature of the attacker, nor can they speculate about what has happened to the six missing ships, seventeen asteroids, one white dwarf star, or all of the blackdragons in the intergalactic region. They have all simply disappeared without a trace.

The StarLeague military is preparing a response. Specially trained cadets will be deployed shortly to combat the incoming threat.

This is The Knowledge, broadcasting from asteroid T-98. Updates will be announced when they become available.

It sounds like it's getting worse. And the rest of the cadets from the military academy are about to be sent into terrible danger. We don't have much time.

I jump out of the ventilation tube, shifting as I fall, landing on the floor on my own two human feet. "Hello!"

The cadets whirl, Tyran hisses in surprise, and Drigo and Rose jump to their feet. Miracle just stares.

Electra rolls her eyes and goes to a drawer set in the wall, pulling out a coverall, which she tosses to me. "Ready to talk, T?"

I pull on the uniform and run a hand over my hair so it's not too messy, because Miracle is watching me curiously. "Yep," I say.

Electra pulls a chair to the table and sits, and I join her. The other cadets leave us to talk, going over to the bunks.

"Tell me what you know," Electra says.

"Commander Io said this room would be monitored," I warn.

Electra makes a scoffing noise. She nods in the direction of the other cadets. "Rose is a communications specialist. We had the cameras and listening devices disabled within five minutes of being put in here."

Cadets! I almost forgot that they're really good at their jobs.

On the table are the leftovers from their lunch. I reach for a half-eaten sandwich and take bites while I talk to Electra.

"I'll tell you what I know, and what I guess," I tell her. There's a pile of protein bars in the middle of the table, so I pull those toward me too. "The first thing I can remember was when I was a blob of goo on the way to the space station, before I ever shifted into my human boy shape. Before I was Trouble."

Electra nods. "That's about the same time that the senior cadets were sent on our mission to recapture you."

"They told you I was a criminal, right?" I ask. "They didn't tell you that I had escaped from a military weapons lab."

"Right," she says. "That part of it was top secret."

Over by the bunks, the other cadets are listening, but that's all right. They need to know all this stuff too.

"Well," I go on, "I knew then that I was trying to escape from something, but I didn't know what. And I knew that I was trying to find something, but I didn't know what that was either."

I remember that feeling. Floating in my blob of goo form in the cold emptiness of space. It makes me shiver. I never want to be that all alone ever again.

My stomach growls, and I unwrap a protein bar and eat it in one bite. "For a long time," I tell Electra, "I assumed that the thing I was running away from was the military weapons lab on the *Peacemaker*. You know."

Electra nods. "The nightmare."

"Yes." I eat another protein bar, not bothering to unwrap it first. "And I thought the thing I was trying to find was Captain Astra—my mom—and the rest of my family and you and a place that would be my home." I shake my head, a very human thing to do. "But I was wrong. I have this feeling that the thing I was running away from is the same as the thing that I am running to."

"What do you mean?" Electra asks.

I sigh. My stomach growls and I reach out and pull a plate toward me and eat it, and then I eat a fork.

Electra stares. "*Trouble!*" she gasps. "Did you just eat a plate?"

"I also ate some socks and boots and engine parts from the *Arrow*, and some old pipes and wires and things, and a big rock and part of a tree while I was at the academy . . ." I try to remember. "Oh, and a whole bunch of pillows."

"You didn't used to do that, did you?" Electra asks. "Eat random things?"

"Nope," I answer.

She frowns. "You're getting hungrier."

"Yep." I stay quiet, waiting for her to figure it out.

When she does, it's like me and Electra are the only two people in the room. She looks straight at me and says softly and seriously, "The threat from the Deep Dark. The Eater. It has something to do with you."

I nod, suddenly feeling nothing at all like the most powerful being in the galaxy, but like a human kid, sort of small and scared. "I thought I was a shapeshifter." I take a shaky breath. "But . . . but . . . Electra, I'm not sure that I'm really a shapeshifter at all. I think I might be something else. Shapeshifting is something that I can *do*, but it's not what I *am*."

43

Keep this in mind. Electra, Miracle, Drigo, Rose, and Tyran. They are kids, but they are also cadets. They are highly trained, weaponized StarLeague soldiers. They are in this room because they want to be. Not because they *have* to be.

Electra leaps up from the table, her eyes blazing. "Commander Io. She *knows*. She knows you have something to do with that Eater. That's why she's been following you."

"I'm not sure what she knows," I answer. "More than I do, anyway." Quickly, I eat three more protein bars, then stuff the rest of them into the pockets of my coverall.

"Think about *this*," Electra says. "You think the StarLeague made you, right? They created the shapeshifter in their military weapons lab." She bangs both hands on the table. "Hah! They didn't create you, T. They *found* you."

"Floating in space," I realize, getting to my feet. "Yes, that's possible."

"Oh, it's possible all right," Electra says. "I'll bet they found you not far from the *Skeleton*."

I've seen Electra angry before, but not like this. She looks like she's about ready to explode. Her fists are clenched and I can see that her tintacles are trying to break out of the head wrap she's wearing. She reaches out and grips me by the shoulder. "Commander Io is going to tell us what's going on. *Now*."

Over by the bunks, Tyran, Miracle, Rose, and Drigo are on their feet.

"We're still with you, weird shapeshifter kid," Miracle Zox says to me. "Even if you're something even weirder than a weird shapeshifter kid."

"That's right," Drigo puts in. "What're your orders, Squad Leader Electra?"

"Tyran!" she snaps. He's already gone to the door, doing something to it so we can escape. The door hisses open, and Miracle Zox holds up a hand. "Let me deal with this," she orders, and then she whirls out into the corridor. By the time I grab the Donut-pillow from the bed and poke my head out, the two StarLeague soldiers who were on guard are disarmed. One of them is lying on the floor at Miracle's feet, clutching a sensitive part of his anatomy; the other is shouting an alert into a wristband that must be a communicator. Miracle Zox, it turns out, is a specialist in close-in fighting.

She's probably almost as dangerous as the Hunter!

"Go ahead and warn Commander Io," Electra snarls as she drags the two soldiers past me into the bunk room. "Tell her we're on our way, and that she's going to tell us the truth about what's going on." Then she grips the front of my coverall, pulls me into the corridor, and hits the button to close the door. Tyran is already at the door controls, making sure it won't open again. Rose and Miracle are looking stupendously competent and alert, holding the guards' blasters.

"Let's go," Electra orders, catching a blaster that Miracle tosses her.

"Which way to the bridge?" Drigo asks, worried.

I spot a scurrying gray shape at the edge of the corridor. "Follow that rat!" I exclaim.

Miracle gives me a look over her shoulder as we all break into a run. "Rats?" she asks. "Really?"

"We're lucky they've decided to help," I answer, and we all race after it, heading for the bridge—the control center of the StarLeague *Arrow*.

This is all very interesting, because usually I am the Hunter and I'm in the lead, but this time I'm happy to carry Donut and let the cadets do all the rawring and stomping around.

The rat leads us to the bridge.

"Thank you!" I say to it as Tyran forces the door open.

Along the way Miracle disarmed a few more soldiers, so they're all carrying blasters.

The rat twitches its whiskers at me, and when I look up, the cadets, led by Miracle, have already stormed onto the bridge, disarmed a couple more soldiers, and gotten the crew members lined up against one wall with their hands or claws raised in surrender. Basically they've taken over the ship. "Well done," Electra says to her sister, who gives her a sharp nod in return, and then Electra is facing the command chair with her fists on her hips. During the brief, fight her tintacles escaped from her wrapper, and they're bright white with fury, writhing around her head.

My best friend! So mighty and wonderful.

Commander Io sits in the chair looking completely unbothered by any of this. She looks past Electra, and when she sees me in the doorway, she nods.

"Hello!" I say to her, and give a half wave.

"Shut up, Trouble," Electra says, glaring at Commander Io. "Don't be nice to her. She doesn't deserve it." She points at a control panel that is blinking and beeping. "Drigo," she orders, without looking around. "Lock that down."

Drigo nods and goes to the panel, where he pushes some buttons. The blinking and beeping stop.

"Now," Electra snaps. "Commander Io. It's time for you to tell Trouble—and us—what you know."

Commander Io studies me for a long moment. The cadets are watching me too, and so are all the crew members.

"You want to know the truth of what you are," Commander Io says to me at last.

I'm about to tell her that I already know what I am—I'm Trouble. But I don't really know anymore. So instead I answer, "Yes. I want to know the truth."

Commander Io nods. "I will tell you where you came from." As she says this, her dark brown eyes seem strangely sad. "And why you are here."

Uh-oh. It's bad, I can tell.

"Electra," I say quietly, because I want to hear this for myself before anybody else knows. "I need to talk to Commander Io alone."

44

"Trouble, *no*," Electra protests. Her tintacles abruptly turn muddy brown. She's very upset that I want her to go away while I talk to Commander Io.

"It's all right," I tell her. "It won't take very long."

Electra makes a low *grrrr* sound. "Fine." She points at the door. "Everybody off the bridge." The crew members and soldiers head out, followed by the cadets.

"Be careful," Electra warns as she steps out, closing the door behind her.

In my hands, the Donut-pillow shifts into its small stone form, and I put it into the pocket of my coverall. Then I cross the shiny metal floor until I reach the control panel nearest to Commander Io's chair. I hop up to sit on it, my legs crisscrossed.

"I have bad dreams," I tell her, "about the military weapons lab."

She winces. "Yes. It was . . . not pleasant." She sighs. "I will tell you what happened and why it happened. Listen carefully. A little over twelve years ago, a StarLeague exploration ship detected an anomaly in the Deep Dark beyond our galaxy. An amorphous intelligence cluster."

"A *what?*" I ask.

"A blob of goo," she explains.

Her answer makes me shiver. *I* am a blob of goo too. At least, I was.

"It was unlike anything we'd ever seen before," she goes on, "and it was enormous. The size of a planetary system. We knew that the crew of the *Skeleton* had disappeared, and our monitoring of the Deep Dark indicated that the blackdragons were disappearing too. We needed to know if the . . . blob . . . was growing larger, if it was a threat. That's when General Smag and the military built the *Peacemaker* and started the cadet program. They thought they would need special military ships and special soldiers to fight the anomaly if it came out of the Deep Dark and into our galaxy. Meanwhile, I was sent in this ship to investigate. When we reached the blob, I sent probes to examine it. They all disappeared." She shakes her head. "We tried communicating with it. It did not respond. The crew of the *Skeleton* was a mystery, however. Why had they been taken but the ship left behind? Some more observations led me to conclude that the blob was not only sentient, but—"

"Sentient?" I ask, not sure what the word means.

"Thinking, feeling," she explains patiently. "A being with its own wishes and needs."

"A giant blobby person," I say.

"Yes," she agrees. "I concluded that the blob was both sentient and curious."

"And hungry," I add. "We call it the Eater."

She gives me an odd look. "The Eater. No. I don't think it took the crew of the *Skeleton* because it was hungry. I think it took them because it wanted to know more about them. So instead of fighting the Eater, as you call it, I decided to try to figure out what it was. And that is when I made a mistake." She takes a deep breath. "You will be right to judge me, Trouble, for what I am about to tell you."

I nod, solemn. "Electra thinks you found me floating in space. But that's not what happened, is it?"

"No," she answers. "I armed the *Arrow* with weapons and left the crew behind. By myself I flew this ship nearer to the blob—the Eater—and fired all the weapons, a huge number of explosives, laser cannons, nuclear blasters. The Eater reacted, and as it did I was able to get close enough to take a sample. And then I fled."

My mouth goes dry. "A sample of the blob," I repeat.

"Yes," she says.

At one end of the bridge is a huge screen that takes up an entire wall. It's showing space. The ship is moving fast because we're on our way to the edge of the galaxy, so stars are flowing by; they look like streaks of bright light against the endless darkness.

Commander Io gets up from the command chair and paces forward to stand where she can see the screen. Without looking around at me, she goes on. "I took the sample—"

"*Not* a sample," I interrupt. "Me. You took *me*."

She nods, still staring at the depths of space. "Yes. I took you to the *Peacemaker*, to the military labs. We needed to find out what you were—what the blob was." She swings around to face me. "We were astonished when we found you, too, were sentient, and when we learned of your shapeshifting ability."

"That's when you tried to turn me into a weapon," I say.

"No." She shakes her head. "That was not our intention. At least, it wasn't mine. Not everyone in the StarLeague agreed about what should be done with you." She sighs. "I am very old, Trouble, and I have been a commander in the StarLeague for a long time. It was once a force for good in this galaxy. It governed, it took care of those who needed help, it protected. But in its fear of the unknown—of the threat from the Deep Dark—it changed. The military part of the government grew more powerful, and then took over. Instead of protecting people across the galaxy, it ruled them. Instead of sending food to those in need, it built weapons and military ships and took children from their families to train them as soldiers. And so, despite my protests, General Smag and his military scientists created the Hunter, as you call it. They also tried splitting you so they could make more Hunters."

"Donut," I say quietly. At her blank look, I add, "The other shapeshifter." I reach into my pocket and pull out Donut, still in the shape of a small stone. "It can only shift into things, not into people. But it is . . ." I try out the new word: "*Sentient*. It's a person."

"I see," Commander Io says. "I hope you will believe that I fought very hard to protect you from the military people."

"It doesn't matter if you fought or not," I tell her. "You gave me to them. And they still did what they did."

"Yes." She puts her hand over her heart and bows to me. "For that I deeply apologize."

I nod. But I don't tell her it's all right. Because it's not. "What did *you* want to do with me?" I ask.

"I hoped we could imprint you with different kinds of beings from our galaxy," she says, "and then send you back as a kind of message for the Eater. If it really was curious, it would have some of its questions answered. It would know that we were people too, and that we didn't want to fight it."

"But I ran away from the military lab on the *Peacemaker*," I say.

"You did." Her wrinkly face relaxes into a smile. "I was very proud of you for that, Trouble, if you can believe it, and proud of you for returning to rescue the other sample—Donut, as you call it." She opens her hand. "I am proud of what you have become."

I shiver, drawing my legs up and encircling them with my arms. What *have* I become? I'm a shapeshifter, and I'm the Hunter, and I'm a human boy, and I'm Electra's best friend, and I'm a really terrible cadet, and I'm Donut's sibling, and

I'm part of a sentient blob from the Deep Dark beyond our galaxy. But most of all, I realize, I'm Captain Astra's kid.

Commander Io climbs back into her command chair. "The blob has invaded our galaxy, eating whatever it encounters. At first it was only the crew of the *Skeleton*, but during the past year it's gotten far worse. It has encroached on the galaxy itself, not far from where we lost the *Skeleton*. We've lost ships, many asteroids, and two white dwarf stars."

I nod. I saw that happen, when the two stars blinked out. When they were *eaten*.

Commander Io goes on. "And now planetary systems are threatened. Let me tell you, Trouble, about what will happen on those planets when the Eater arrives. One second the sun is shining, all is well. The next, the envelope of air around the planet—the atmosphere—boils away. To the people on the planet there will be a moment where the sky goes dark before the entire planet—all its people and wildlife and trees and mountains and ocean—blinks out of existence. There is no escape. We cannot get there in time to evacuate the people who live on those planets. The Eater will be there first. And I think I know why."

I shiver, thinking of all those people on those planets, in such terrible danger. "It must be searching for me," I say slowly. "Or . . . not for me, exactly. For the bit of blob that you took from it. The sample."

"Yes," Commander Io says. "And now you know what you truly are. You were not made to be a weapon, Trouble." She sighs wearily. "You were made to be a hero."

When she says this, I get a horrible empty, sinking feeling in my stomach, and it's not hunger.

I know what Commander Io is saying, and I know why she looks so sad.

I was made to be a hero, she said.

Do you know what that means? What it *really* means?

"I am sorry to ask this of you, Trouble," Commander Io says, "but the fate of the galaxy is at stake. We don't have much time. We will arrive at the last known location of the Eater very soon. You must—"

"I know," I say sadly, because I can't let planets die. "I know what has to be done."

And I tell her that I will do it.

But, I tell her, I want one thing first.

I want to say goodbye to my mom.

45

I know that Captain Astra will never leave me behind.

Commander Io says, "We don't know where the *Hindsight* is located. We lost track of them after you went to the academy at Apex-9. We may not have enough time to find them before the Eater reaches the planetary system that it is threatening."

And I say, "Hah!" and hop off the control panel that I've been sitting on. I know my mom, and I know the *Hindsight* is around here somewhere. I bet it's hidden, thanks to a stealth-box or the blackdragon; Captain Astra has been following the *Arrow* the same way the *Arrow* followed us.

I go over to the door of the bridge. Then I pause. What am I going to tell Electra?

Lying didn't taste very good. I'm not doing that again.

If anybody's going to understand what I have to do, it'll be Electra. But I have to talk to Captain Astra first.

I hit the button and the door swishes open; on the other side is our squad. At a nod from Electra, Tyran, Drigo, and Rose hurry onto the bridge and go to different stations; Miracle Zox stands guard by the door. "Tell them to stop the ship," I say to Electra, and she snaps out an order. A moment later the screen at the end of the room shows the stars settling back into their places as the *Arrow* slows and then stops.

"There's no sign of another ship," Rose reports.

"That's all right," I answer. "The *Hindsight* is out there."

As Commander Io comes over to join us, I say to Electra, "I'm going to talk to Captain Astra. I'll tell you everything when I get back."

Electra gives a curt nod. "You'd better."

Commander Io says, "Trouble, you can use the shuttle to fly over to the *Hindsight*, assuming it really is here. I can provide a pilot."

Ever since I first took my human boy shape I have wanted to roll my eyes at something. Captain Astra does it all the time. It's such a wonderfully human way of saying, *That is the dumbest thing I've ever heard!* Commander Io wants me to fly to the *Hindsight* on a shuttle? I give her the rolliest of eyerolls and then shift into my Hunter shape.

Waving a claw at Io and Electra—*Byeeee*—I pick up my coverall, with Donut in the pocket, and lope off the bridge until I reach the nearest airlock. Stepping in, I close the inner hatch behind me, open the outer hatch, and am sucked out into the frozen darkness of space.

And of course the *Hindsight* is there, just like it was after I rescued Donut from General Smag's ship. My mom always finds me. On the way I see the blackdragon, still wrapped around the end of the ship. There's nobody to meet me at the *Hindsight*'s outer hatch, but as I get closer, it opens, welcoming me inside. Once the hatch is sealed behind me, I shift into my human boy shape, put on the coverall, and with my stomach growling I go down the corridor until I reach the mess-room. The door is open, and I peer in.

The mess-room is just as colorful as ever, and messier, since I haven't been here to keep it clean. It smells like engine oil and dirty socks and spices. It smells like home.

The captain is sitting at the table with her back to me. "I don't *know* why they stopped," she's saying to Fred, who's in the galley. A moment later Reetha comes in the other door—she must have opened the outer hatch to let me in. She catches the captain's eye and points a claw at me.

Captain Astra whirls around.

I haven't been gone for that long—maybe two weeks—but I have missed my mom so, so much. Most of the time I was too busy to think about it, but now that I'm home, all of the missing hits me at once, and I suddenly feel shaky and full of happiness, but also terrible sadness.

"*Trouble*," the captain breathes. She closes her eyes for a moment, then gets to her feet and crosses the room to me. She wraps me in a hug and I lean against her and feel safe and comforted, the way any kid feels when they see their mom after a long time away.

Then she takes me by the shoulders and glares down at me. "*Never* do that again." She means *never run away from home like that.*

I can't say *I won't* because I'm about to do something even worse. "I need to talk to you," I say instead. Then my stomach growls loudly.

She snorts out a laugh. "Come on, kiddo," she says, turning back to the mess-room.

Fred, standing at the table, gives me a sharp-toothed scowl. "We've been very worried about you," he complains.

"Sorry," I say, surprised. I figured he'd be glad I was gone!

"Well," he says grumpily, "the captain is right. Don't do it again."

Reetha is staring at me with her golden eyes. "Follow. *Arrow*?" she asks.

"Yes," I answer, and then glance at Captain Astra. "If it's all right. Electra's still over there."

"I'm sure you have a very good explanation for all of this," she says to me, and then waves a weary hand at Reetha. "Yeah, follow them for now."

A nod, and Reetha and Fred leave.

I go straight to the galley and get out six noodle packets and the bright orange cheese powder. I poke my head out. "Kaff?" I ask.

"For the past two weeks I've been *living* on kaff," Captain Astra says with a sigh, settling into her favorite chair at the table.

Because she's been worried about me, I know. It's not going to get any better, so I don't say anything. Instead I make five bowls of noodles and neon cheese for me and one for her and carry them all out to the table. Handing her a fork, I sit down and start eating.

"So," she says, twirling a bite of noodles around her fork and blowing on it to cool it. "You went to help Electra?"

I finish my first bowl of noodles and start slurping up the second. "Sort of," I answer between bites. I start on the third bowl.

"And?" Captain Astra asks.

Oop, I ate my fork by accident. Hoping my mom didn't notice, I get up, go to the galley to get another one, sit back down, and start on the fourth bowl of noodles. "Electra went to the StarLeague academy to rescue her sister."

"On Apex-9," she says impatiently. "I know. We followed the *Arrow*."

Oh, that's right. Um. "I had to pretend to be a cadet."

Captain Astra rolls her eyes, which makes me laugh. "I'm sure *that* went well," she comments.

"I set a new record for number of faults in one day," I say, and then add, "The cadets are given faults when they get into trouble."

"Which you are very good at," she puts in.

"Yep," I say, and finish the last of my noodles and neon cheese.

"Done?" the captain asks with an edge in her voice.

"For now," I answer with a happy sigh.

"Good," she says. "Now quit stalling, kiddo, and tell me what in all of rat-bit space is going on, because it's more than Electra and her sister and the StarLeague academy."

I'm full of food and wonderfully warm, and I'm so glad to be home, and yes, there's some big awful things that we need to talk about, but I've just realized that I can't even remember the last time I slept. I get up from the table and flop onto the blue-and-green patterned couch. My human eyes drop closed.

Go ahead and ask your questions, Mom. I'll answer them.

Later.

46

When I open my eyes, there's a rat sitting on
my chest, peering into my face.

"Hello," I say in a voice crackly with sleep.

The rat twitches his whiskers at me.

While I was sleeping, Donut shifted into its fuzzy blanket
form and covered me up, so I'm warm and cozy. And hungry, of course. The mess-room is dark—it's the middle of the
night, ship time—and Captain Astra is sprawled in her chair
with her feet up on another chair. She's not asleep; she's staring up at the ceiling.

She doesn't know that rats are the most intelligent lifeform in the galaxy, so I'm surprised she's not jumping to her
feet yelling, *Gah! Rat!*

Carefully, I sit up, and the rat moves to perch on my knee.

"The blackdragon is still out there," the captain says softly.

"Yep." The blackdragon is still wrapped around one end of our tin-can-shaped ship. It's singing, but its song is so deep and low that my human ears can't hear it except for an almost indetectable hum that blends with the sound of the usual ship noises.

"I think I've been listening to blackdragons for a long time," she says. "I always thought it was the singing of the stars, but it was them, all along. Blackdragons singing from beyond the edge of the galaxy." She's quiet for a moment. "It's a lonely sound."

"It's not as lonely as it was before," I say. "Now that it's with us."

"Good," she says.

It makes me realize that my captain really is a little like a blackdragon. She likes the dark, quiet places between stars. And I think she used to be lonely too.

"While you were napping," she says, "Electra and your other friends on the *Arrow* contacted us. They're on their way over here in the shuttle." Abruptly, she sits up and plants her feet on the floor with a *thump*. "Which means as soon as they get here, it's time for some explaining. In the meantime, this *rat* wants to talk to you, since apparently that's a thing that rats do."

The rat scampers off my knee and over the floor and up a leg of the table to the tabletop, where it noses the remote, the controller for the screen that takes up part of one wall of the mess-room.

Setting Donut aside, trying to ignore my growling stomach, I get to my feet. The captain swivels in her chair so she can see. The rat peers at the remote, and with one of its front paws it presses a button, scrolls through some information, and then presses another button.

Greetings, says a deep voice, and the screen goes a bright white.

"Hello, The Knowledge!" I say. "It's been a long time since we saw you. Are you all right?"

The bright white screen pulses, making a deep humming noise. *No being has ever asked The Knowledge that question before.*

"Because nobody wanted to know," the captain mutters. She had a bad experience with The Knowledge and doesn't like it much.

There is knowledge, The Knowledge says. *The rats insist that it be shared with you, Trouble.*

"The rats," Captain Astra interrupts with a snort.

The Knowledge ignores her. *You are aware of the anomaly, the amorphous intelligence cluster.*

I glance over at Captain Astra to see if I can tell what she already knows about this. She's frowning as she looks at me, meeting my eyes.

This is going to be hard for her. It's hard for me too. But no more lying—that's what I decided. She's my mom. She needs to know. I'll tell Electra, too, when she gets here, if Commander Io hasn't already filled her in.

"It's a giant blob," I tell my mom. "From the Deep Dark.

It's coming into our galaxy looking for me because it's where I came from. I was a sample taken from the blob by the StarLeague."

As an answer, Captain Astra gets to her feet, kicks her chair over, stalks to the other end of the room muttering something that sounds like curses and *StarLeague*, comes back, and stands with her arms crossed, staring at the screen. "Is all of that true?" she asks The Knowledge.

It is, it tells her.

She swings around to face me. "So we have to help you escape from this blob thing."

The Hindsight, The Knowledge interrupts, *and the StarLeague* Arrow *are approaching the last known location of the* blob, *as you call it.*

"What?" Captain Astra says with a shake of her head. "No. We have to turn the ship around."

"I can't escape from it," I say, and my stomach growls loudly. "For one thing, the StarLeague is about to send the cadets on a mission to fight it, and I can't let that happen because they'll all die. For another, the blob is eating things. It ate the crew of the *Skeleton*, and two white dwarf stars, and a bunch of asteroids, and it's about to eat some planets that people live on."

As I say the words, I suddenly understand what Commander Io meant when she called me a *shapeshifter bomb*. I haven't eaten a star or a spaceship crew, but I have eaten a boulder, engine parts, all kinds of junk, and a lot of pillows.

And I'm only getting hungrier.

"There's more, isn't there?" I ask The Knowledge. "There's something else about me, and about the blob." I take a step closer to the screen. "Tell me."

"Trouble, *stop*," Captain Astra protests.

"Mom," I say, my voice shaking. "I have to know."

I hear her take a ragged breath. But she doesn't say anything.

"You know everything," I say to the Knowledge. "Tell us what you know about me."

The screen pulses white, and when The Knowledge speaks, its voice is as deep and emotionless as it always is. *As you know, Trouble, you emit what we thought was a unique energy when you shift from one shape to another. It is how the StarLeague was able to track you across the galaxy—every time you shifted, you emitted the energy signal.*

I nod. I've known about this for a long time.

The blob, as you call it, emits the same energy signal. But the signal is not *unique, as we thought before. The Knowledge has been monitoring, cataloging, sorting, identifying, analyzing, and recording every signal emitted by every energy source in the entire galaxy.*

"You did that for me?" I interrupt.

Yes, The Knowledge responds. *It was a task worthy of my vast intelligence.*

The rat is still sitting on the table. It squeaks loudly.

It was the rats' idea, The Knowledge admits.

The captain comes over and puts a hand on my shoulder and speaks to The Knowledge. "Just tell us what this energy signal *is*, you overgrown asteroid rat-collaborator."

By applying certain filters, it was possible to ascertain that the energy is given off by another intergalactic phenomenon, one that is relatively common, though not in the form observed. The energy ranges from—

"What?" I interrupt. "Just tell me—what am I?"

The Knowledge pauses before answering.

In the silence, my stomach growls loudly.

You, Trouble, The Knowledge intones, *are a black hole.*

47

It's hard for the brains of people like you and me to understand how truly huge the universe is.

It's huge and unending and expanding, and also full of many, many strange things. There are so many planets in the universe that you could start counting them now and not be done counting them for a million years. There are comets that take long, lonely trips around those planets, trailing tails of burning dust. There are warm red giant stars, ordinary yellow stars like the sun of human Earth, blue stars that burn the brightest, and there are twirling twin binary stars. There are asteroids and planetoids and moons; there are supernovas and pulsars and there are nebulas, which are vast clouds of dust and gas where baby stars are born. There are galaxies like this one—so many galaxies that to the universe they're like stars sprinkled across a velvet darkness that goes on forever.

In all the entire universe, the strangest thing might be me. Because I *am* a kid.

And . . . I am a black hole.

Ordinary black holes are stars that implode until they have so much gravity that they suck everything in, even light. That's why they're black—no light escapes from them. Black holes are huge, hungry beasts.

The Knowledge explains that the Eater is something completely new. It's a black hole that is *sentient*. That means it's a person. It was wandering around the universe until it came to our galaxy, and maybe Commander Io is right. Maybe it *was* curious. But then a piece of it was taken away, and it's been trying to find that piece—me—for the last twelve years.

"Well," I say to Captain Astra, "I guess that explains why I'm hungry all the time."

She's sitting in her chair with her elbows on her knees and her head in her hands.

"Because," I go on, "there's a black hole inside me."

"Yes, Trouble," she says, her voice muffled. "I get it."

The Knowledge is still on the screen; the rat is on the table watching, its whiskers twitching.

Your black hole, Trouble, The Knowledge explains in its deep voice, *is infinitesimally small. No bigger than a molecule. Yet it contains tremendous power.*

"The Eater must be a lot bigger," I say.

Yes, The Knowledge says. *It is a super-massive black hole, even more powerful than the black hole at the center of this galaxy.*

It keeps talking, going on about the size of the Eater and its unusual blobular covering, and its strange way of traveling through space, and the possible fate of whatever it has eaten—it uses the word *spaghettification*, which I've never heard of before—but I don't pay it much attention.

Because I'm listening for the sound of the *Hindsight*'s pulse engines, and I can't hear them. The ship has stopped because we've reached the edge of the galaxy. Then I hear a *bump* and a *thump*, which means Electra's shuttle has arrived from the *Arrow* and has glommed on to our ship's outer hatch. She'll be here in a minute.

I go over to stand in front of Captain Astra's chair.

She scrubs her hands through her curly gray hair and slowly gets to her feet. "So this blob," she says. "The wandering black hole. The Eater. We can't run away from it."

"Nope," I tell her. "I think it would end up eating everything in the entire galaxy to get me back." And then I add the part about the *shapeshifter bomb*. "It's dangerous, and I'm dangerous too. The black hole in me is getting hungrier. I think I would end up eating everything I could too. Even this ship, even though it's my home."

She nods, understanding. Her face is so, so tired. It's wrinklier than it used to be. She's unhappier than she ever was before. I wish she didn't have to end up alone.

I'm suddenly so full of sadness that tears spill out of my eyes. "I'm sorry," I say to her. "I'm glad you were my mom."

She reaches out and puts her hands on my shoulders. "No

matter what happens, Trouble," she says quietly, "I will always be your mom. And you will always be my kid." She leans forward and kisses my forehead.

And then something extremely weird happens.

48

Alert! **The Knowledge blares.** *The anomaly approaches the approximate position of the* Hindsight! *It is the blob! The Eater! Prepare to retreat! Alert!* it repeats. *Alert!*

My mom straightens and starts to turn.

The rat squeaks and jumps off the edge of the table.

The door to the corridor whooshes opens and Electra strides in, followed by Tyran and her sister, Miracle.

My stomach gives a ferocious growl.

The lights flicker.

And then everything stops.

The screen goes blank white and The Knowledge says a groaning *Eaterrrrrr* and falls silent.

I know what this is. The Eater—the black hole—must be very close. It's bending space around it. Time has stopped.

Captain Astra stands mid-turn, one hand still on my shoulder, her mouth open to say something.

The rat hangs in the air, caught in mid-jump between the table and the floor.

Electra, Miracle, and Tyran are frozen, the door half-closed behind them.

I take a slow breath. Then another. With my sleeve I wipe the tears off my face.

Carefully, I duck out from under Captain Astra's hand and go to the couch, where Donut has shifted into its small, shiny stone form. I pick it up. "The Eater is here," I tell it, and then shiver, because my voice sounds so tiny in the dead air, and I'm really, truly scared, maybe for the first time in my entire life.

But I'm determined, too.

You know how I can never tell what Reetha is thinking because she's a lizardian and I'm usually in a human shape, and lizardian brains are just too different for human brains to understand?

Well, I'm guessing the Eater is like that, except a million times more different.

It is sentient and it has been searching for me, right? Maybe not right. It's been searching for the sample that was stolen from it, but it might not even know that there's a *me*.

What I'm afraid of is that the Eater will take me back, and I will become part of it, and I won't be *me* anymore.

But you know what? I'm not going to let that happen without a fight.

A deep, rumbling-humming noise has started so that the floor is shivering under my feet as I hurry to the galley. My stomach growls loudly as I jerk open the cupboards and start eating.

I eat everything.

And I mean *everything*. I eat the dishes, forks, spoons, all the salad *and* the dirt it grows in, all the food, including the packaging, and about forty-two protein bars.

My stomach—the black hole inside me, I mean—gives a warning grumble. That was a lot to eat, but it still wasn't enough to eat. It's like as the Eater gets closer, I get hungrier.

Gobbling down one last fork, I step out into the mess-room again.

Captain Astra, Electra, the rat, Miracle, Tyran, all still frozen.

It's likely that I will never see them again. "Goodbye," I say sadly, even though they probably can't hear me.

The rumbling-humming noise gets louder. I'd better get off the *Hindsight* before the Eater eats it and my family and my squad get spaghettified, whatever that means. Squished and stretched out for eternity, maybe.

The entire ship is rattling as I race through the corridor to the hatch. I step in and hit the button to close the inner hatch.

There in the airlock I take Donut out of my pocket and hold it in my hand. "It's time," I tell it. I wonder if it's as scared as I am.

I'm about to shift into the Hunter form so I can leave the *Hindsight* and go out and fight the Eater, if that's even possible, when the outer hatch slams open . . .

. . . and in my human boy shape I'm sucked out of the ship and into deepest space.

49

Do you remember about *ebullism*? It's what happens when a person who's not wearing a space suit gets sucked out of a ship. Gruesome, explodey death, that's what ebullism is.

But that's not what happens to me.

I'm pulled out of the *Hindsight* and go whirling into the emptiness, tumbling over and over until the flying turns to falling and I crash-land face-first on a hard surface—*ow!* As I hit, Donut pops out of my hand and goes rattling away. I take a shuddering breath. And another one. Well, I'm not ebullismized, at least. And there's air to breathe. I open my eyes. I'm lying on a floor that I know very well because I have scrubbed it many times. Squinting, I see the leg of a table. And chair legs. And a couch with a blue-and-green patterned cover.

Carefully, I climb to my feet.

I'm standing in a place that looks like the mess-room of the *Hindsight*, except that it has no walls and no ceiling. The floor is a platform floating in a vast, empty, dark space. If I stepped off the edge into the nothingness, I'd fall for a long, long time. Assuming there's gravity out there.

Well, there *is* gravity out there. I must be inside the Eater; I'm inside a sentient black hole, the ultimate gravity in the universe, so powerful it even sucks in light.

Creepy.

The Eater must have made a bubble of safety for me—this platform that looks like the coziest place in my home on the *Hindsight*. I figure that's a good sign. Still, I shiver and look around the platform for Donut. It's under the captain's favorite chair, still in the shape of a rock. I go over and pick it up and slip it into my pocket, where it will be safe.

Safe-ish.

Not safe at all, really.

The Eater must have brought me here for a reason. If Commander Io was right about the Eater, I think I know what its reason is.

Staring out at the empty darkness, I spy a tiny point of light shooting toward me. It gets closer, traveling fast. As it slows, nearing the platform, I realize that it is a small blob. It is a piece of the Eater.

Against the deep darkness, the blob is shimmery, like an amoeba, and it's about the size of a large rat.

It hovers at the edge of the platform, and I know what it is doing—it's examining me with its blob senses.

It is *curious*.

"Hello, Eater," I say, and give half a wave.

At the sound of my voice, the blob flinches back, and then it blurs and changes and steps onto the mess-room platform, joining me in my bubble of safety.

The Eater is a giant blob and it's a black hole, and it is also a shapeshifter. It has taken the shape of a kid who looks exactly like me. A skinny human boy with pale skin and brown hair. Only the eyes are different. Its eyes are so black that they seem to have no bottom, like the deepest reaches of space. Its eyes suck in the light—that's how dark they are.

I stand facing the Eater. "Hello," I say again. And I add, to be polite to the most powerful being in the universe, "Nice to meet you."

My stomach growls loudly, almost as if it's saying hello to the Eater too.

Well, maybe it *is*. The tiny black hole inside me greeting another black hole.

The Eater is studying me with its endlessly dark eyes. Its face is blank. "Interesting," it says in a halting voice. Like this: In. Ter. Est. Ing.

Maybe it's not used to talking out loud.

"What's interesting?" I ask.

The Eater steps closer to me.

My stomach answers with a loud rumble.

"What . . . is it," the Eater says, cocking its head, studying me.

"I'm Trouble." I point to my stomach. "I have a black hole inside me, and it gives me my shapeshifter power, but really I'm just a kid."

"A strange concept," the Eater says in its hollow voice. "Separate. Identities."

It's *so* weird to hear it talking with my mouth. I also don't understand what it means. "Separate identities?" I ask.

"The idea," it goes on. "That there is a *you*. That is separate from a *me*." When I shake my head, still not getting it, the Eater goes on. "There is no *you*. There is only *me*."

"There is too a me," I tell it. "I'm right here, standing in front of you."

"You believe . . ." It pauses. "It believes it has. A distinct. Self," the Eater says.

"You believe it too," I tell it. "You just called me *you*. We're two different people. You're the Eater. I'm a kid named Trouble." I dig into my pocket and pull out the stone. "And this is Donut. It's a person too." Carefully, I set Donut on the floor, where it will be safe-ish.

The Eater doesn't blink. It just stares at me with its endless eyes. "Well then," it says. "*You* were taken from *me*. *I* want *you* back."

"I don't want to go back," I tell it. "I like it out here."

"Fascinating," the Eater says. "But not—" For the first time it gets an expression on its blank face. It frowns. The

Eater's human boy skin ripples and turns the deep, furry black of a blackdragon. The Eater waves a hand and its skin shifts back to its usual pale color. A second later, its hair turns purple and two insectoid antennae sprout from its head. At the same time, the Eater's human hand turns into a furry dog puppy paw. "Oop," it says.

"What's the matter?" I ask it.

"Hungry," it answers. Its starless dark eyes are fixed on me. A deep, rumbling sound fills the platform and fades away. A stomach growling, except the stomach is the size of a supermassive black hole.

Uh-oh. Commander Io was right about the Eater. It is curious. But it's also the hungriest being in the entire universe. I hoped maybe the curiosity would win out, and it would leave me—and the galaxy—alone. But it looks like the hunger is winning.

I know what the Eater eats.

Me.

50

The Eater—shaped like me but with purple hair, antennae, and one furry paw—stalks toward me. Its black-hole stomach rumbles again, and the air ripples and the floor under my feet trembles.

I growl and show my teeth, which would be a lot scarier if I wasn't in my human boy shape.

"Hungry," the Eater repeats, and takes another step closer. It stamps the floor, and the entire platform shakes. "A piece of me was taken. I want myself back!" It reaches for me. "Huuuuuuunnnnnnngryyyyyy," it growls.

Using the power of the tiny black hole that is inside me, I shift into the form of the Hunter.

Rawr! I roar, ready to fight. *You can't have me!*

In response, the Eater's arms shift into massive metallic claws. It stalks across the floor, clashing the claws together until they crackle with electric energy. A bolt of that power arcs across the space between us. As it reaches me I use my Hunter speed to blur aside, and the bolt goes sizzling out into the emptiness beyond the platform. I blur to the side again and spit out a glob of acid, which I hurl at the Eater. The acid splatters across its front and it howls in surprise, and its eyes pop out into eyestalks and its hair bursts into flame. The platform echoes and shakes with the thunderous sound of its stomach growling.

It paces toward me. With each step it grows larger and its body changes. First its human boy skin turns into insectoid carapace—armor. Then its mouth widens and bristling fangs erupt from its jaws. It opens its mouth wide—wider—and I can see the seething darkness of its black hole down there, hungry to swallow me up. It lurches closer, growing to three times my size, crackling all over with electric flames.

I crouch, ready to defend myself.

The Eater reaches out for me and starts to take another step, when part of the floor shifts, turning into a heavy chain that flings itself around its lower legs and tightens, anchoring the Eater so it can't move. Donut! So brave!

As the Eater turns to snarl down at the chain imprisoning it, I move with blinding speed, darting behind it, jumping onto its back, putting a razor-sharp claw across its neck. *I am me, I am not you!* I roar at it. *I am Trouble! Let me go!*

Under my claws, the Eater shifts—insectoid, lizardian with gleaming golden eyes, giant tentacle-fang creature, squirming dog puppy—and I hang on through all of it until it shifts into the form of a military weapons scientist with a white coat and masked face—the shape of my nightmares—and I *know* it's not real, but I flinch, and that gives the Eater time to fling me off. I go tumbling across the platform to the very edge of the darkness.

The Eater kicks off the Donut-chain, turns, and takes a step toward me. The roar of its hunger echoes around us. Suddenly it shifts again and its carapace, its metal claws, the flames, all of it melts away, leaving behind the outline of a boy, but filled with empty black space that is howlingly, achingly hungry.

Quickly, I shift back into my own boy shape and put on the coverall that was left behind on the floor when I shifted into the Hunter.

Then I stand and face the kid-shaped black hole that is the Eater.

It stops and reaches out a hand—and its shadowy arm grows longer and longer, stretching out to me, ready to dig for the tiny black hole inside me.

And I feel its power, a power bigger than a galaxy, the most powerful force in the entire universe. Compared to the Eater, my own black-hole power is the tiniest spark. There is nothing I can do to stop it. It's going to eat me and I'll be gone forever.

Still, I back up to the very edge of the platform, with the emptiness behind me and the Eater stretching out taller and taller and leaning hungrily over me. Black tendrils erupt from its head and shoulders and wrap around me. They're icy cold, freezing my skin wherever they touch, and I start to shiver.

But still I push back with every scrap of my being, closing my eyes so I can't see the darkness that surrounds me. No. I am *me*. I am *Trouble*. You can't have me! With my entire self I hold on to my spark of power. But I can feel myself weakening, growing cold. The icy bands of darkness tighten around me. Thunder roars. My spark flickers, about to go out.

And then, from the other end of the platform, comes a dry-voiced question. "Trouble," my mom asks, "what in all of rat-bit space is going on here?"

51

My eyes pop open.

The Eater drops me and I flop onto the floor, on my hands and knees, coughing as the Eater whirls, its tentacles of icy darkness whipping around its head.

Blinking, I see my mom, with Electra, Miracle, and Tyran, stepping onto the platform. All of them look fierce and competent and determined, and I'm very glad to see them.

"Hello," I croak.

And I'm also terrified that they're here, because they're *people* who are *inside* a *black hole* and the Eater is going to kill them and then devour me, and I really don't want them to be dead if they don't have to be.

"What are you doing here?" I gasp.

"Shut up, T," Electra snaps. Her eyes are fixed on the Eater, and she's crouched, ready to take action. "Drigo and

Rose are on the shuttle as backup, waiting to pick us up." She points toward the darkness, but I can't see any shuttle out there. "We're here to rescue you."

"We're cadets, dummy," Miracle says to me.

"We were trained for this," Tyran adds.

They were trained for facing down the most powerful being in the universe with a couple of blasters? I don't think so.

"And apparently I'm the brains of this brainless operation," Captain Astra adds.

The Eater is all writhing black-hole hunger-tentacles at the edge of the platform, but it's waiting—watching. It's curious.

"How—" I ask, wobbling to my feet. "How did you fly the shuttle here?"

Captain Astra points into the darkness. "Blackdragon. Turns out it can travel inside a black hole. Apparently, it's part of the . . ." She glances aside at Electra. "The what was it?"

"The blackdragon is a kid, right?" Electra says briskly. "It is part of our squad."

"That makes total sense," I say.

"It does?" Captain Astra asks.

"Less talking," Miracle puts in, "more rescuing."

"You ready to go, T?" Electra asks.

"I don't think—" I start to say, when the Eater makes its move.

All its curiosity has been eaten up again, by its huge hunger. "*Less talking*," it howls, "*and more eating*." With a ravenous screech, it leaps to the center of the platform, the floor cracking under its feet. Electra gives a signal, and she and Miracle dart to one corner of the platform while Tyran goes to another. They all train their weapons on the Eater, while Captain Astra stumbles backward. But she's too slow—the Eater's tentacles whip out and wrap around her, dragging her closer.

It's going to eat her! "No!" I shout, and race across the floor until I push past the ice-cold, clinging tentacles, putting myself between Captain Astra and the Eater.

Electra and the other cadets are firing their blasters, but the bolts are being sucked in by the black hole—they have no effect at all on the Eater.

I can feel Captain Astra's hands on my shoulders, steadying me as I face the seething, tentacled, black-hole boy shape. "Stop shooting!" I yell at Electra, and the blaster fire stops. "You can't have her!" I shout at the Eater. "This is my mom."

The Eater pauses, because it is massively powerful and dangerous and alien—and it can't resist its own curiosity. Its black-hole tentacles writhe around it, and it's barely human shaped anymore. "*Mom?*" it howls. "What is *Mom?*"

"My mom takes care of me," I tell it.

"Ah," the Eater says, looming over me. "I am *Mom.*"

"No," I tell it, and I don't have a single doubt that what I'm saying is completely true. "My mom loves me, and she wants me to be me. You want me to be you. It's not the same."

The Eater gives a thundering roar and then bends over me, all icy tentacles and darkness, and howls right into my face, "*HUNGRY.*"

I can feel Captain Astra trying to pull me away, and I can hear that Electra and the rest of the squad have started firing their weapons again, but I stand there looking into the endless black hole that is the Eater as it lets my mom go and wraps its tentacles around me.

Here's the thing.

I'm a shapeshifter. I know what it's like to see things as someone else. Weirdly, seeing the Eater like this—so ravenously hungry—makes me feel not afraid anymore, but . . . sorry for it. Part of it was taken away. It wants that part back. I know what it's like to be hungry, and also to want something so much that I will do anything to get it.

"Wait!" I shout. "I have an idea!" I take a gasping breath, because the tentacles are squeezing me tightly. "Don't you want to know what it is? Aren't you curious?"

And just like before, on the *Hindsight*, everything stops as the Eater bends space-time around us.

Electra, Miracle, Tyran, all unmoving, and blaster bolts frozen halfway across the platform. My mom behind me, eyes closed, bracing herself, frozen while trying to pull the tentacles away from me.

And the Eater, suddenly letting me go, shrinking down into the outline of a human boy, blurry around the edges, black hole everywhere else. "Curious," it says. And then it adds, "*Hungry*." Its voice is more controlled, but still with an edge of that ravenous howl.

"I know," I tell it, and I take a shivery breath, steadying myself. I hope this is going to work. "I think . . . I think I know what we can do." I step closer to the Eater, only an arm's length away. "Do you understand that you are you and I am me?"

"No. That is me," the Eater answers. It points at me. At my stomach, to be specific.

I nod. Here's my idea. "Can you take it back? Just the black hole part that is you, and leave the me part behind?"

It goes still. Sentient, powerful, unlike anything else in the universe.

It doesn't have eyes, exactly, but somehow I can tell that all of its huge self is focused on me, and it makes me feel so tiny that I wonder if it can even see me.

"You *are* you," it says slowly, almost wonderingly. "Yes." It reaches out a black-hole hand, and I can feel it pulling at the tiny spark of black hole inside me. To my surprise, I can feel that my own black hole *wants* to go. It's just as hungry to get back to the place where it came from, to its *self*.

Then the Eater stops. "When I am whole again, it will . . . *you* will lose your ability to change shape," it says. "Do you wish to take another form before I take your power?"

I blink, surprised. The Eater is letting me choose. Is it being . . . *nice*? For half a second I think about myself as the Hunter, hugely powerful, or as an adorable dog puppy, or as a Tintaclodian like Electra. But none of those are who I really am.

"No," I say. "I like being a human kid."

"And that." The Eater points again. It's pointing at a small stone shape lying on the floor only four steps away. Donut. "That one too," the Eater says. "That is me. Is it also a you?"

I nod. "It's Donut. Its own person." I go over and pick Donut up, holding it in my hand. I realize what losing its power will mean. It will have to stay in the same shape forever. "Do you want to go back to the Eater?" I ask it. "Or stay with us?"

As an answer, Donut shifts. It takes the shape of a purple-and-yellow stripy pillow with silky fringes around the edges, pom-poms at each corner, and a brand-new scattering of shiny golden sequins over its surface. It wants to stay.

"All right," I tell the Eater, hugging the Donut-pillow to me. My mom and Electra and the rest are still frozen, with no idea what's going on. "We're ready. Do it. Do it now."

The Eater reaches out. Its howling darkness surrounds me and Donut. It is icy cold and hot at the same time and windy and thunderingly loud, and then, suddenly, it's silent.

Fwip! A tiny black hole zips out of Donut.

And *fwip!* My own black hole zips out of me and disappears into the Eater—back home where it belongs.

52

Electra, Miracle, and Tyran are unfrozen, standing at one end of the platform. The blackdragon is hovering nearby, almost invisible against the darkness, wrapped around the shuttle, ready to take us back to the *Hindsight*.

Captain Astra and I are standing in the middle of the platform talking to the most powerful being in the entire universe, who has taken the form of a blob of goo not much bigger than I am.

I am a human boy, and I feel very strange. Different. But I can't think about that now.

"You'll have to give back all the things you ate," I tell the Eater.

Already did, it tells us. It doesn't make itself any tongue and teeth to speak with; it just opens a weird mouth in its goo and the words come out. Somehow it looks plump and happy.

Well, it has the missing parts of itself back again—the tiny black holes that were in me and Donut. It's not hungry anymore. Maybe it *is* happy.

"So you gave everything back?" I ask the Eater. "The crew of the *Skeleton* and the asteroids and the stars and the black-dragons, and everything?"

Yes, the Eater says. *But you,* it adds. *Trouble. You are still mine.*

I get a sinking feeling in my stomach. Uh-oh. I thought we settled this.

This is your mom, the Eater says, and a pseudopod points at Captain Astra.

"I am," she answers.

I am also your mom, the Eater says. *You are my child.*

"Uhhhhh," is all I can think of to say. What?

Beside me, Captain Astra bursts out laughing.

I need a mom name, it tells me. *I do not like* Eater. *Do not call me that.*

"Wow," I say, because coming up with a name for an ultra-massively-powerful sentient black hole? Not easy!

And then it makes it easy.

Wow, it repeats. *Yes. It is like* Mom *but upside-down. That will be my name. Wow.*

So I have a mom.

And I have a wow.

Families! So complicated!

I say goodbye to Wow. It tells me that it is curious about animals and plants and planets and things that are sentient and colorful and warm and alive—most of space is cold and airless and boring and *not* alive, it tells me, which I know already. It also says it might want me to do some things for it, once I've gotten used to being a human kid and not a shapeshifter. I promise to come back to visit it soon at the edge of the galaxy.

"Come *on*," Miracle yells across the platform at me. As I go over to join the rest of our squad and my mom, she turns to her sister. "Does Trouble always do this?"

"Do what?" Electra asks.

"Make people like him?" Miracle asks. "Even when the people are giant black-hole blob things?"

I grin at Miracle, because I like her. A *lot*.

"Yes," Electra says, with an eyeroll. "He does."

Then we all climb onto the shuttle and the kid blackdragon swoops out of the darkness and gathers us up in its beautiful dark coils to take us back to the *Hindsight*. As we fly to the edge of the galaxy where our ship is waiting, the blackdragon starts to sing. Its song is a deep, thrumming sound, and it's not sad anymore, or lonely, because from all around us comes the sound of other blackdragons, freed from the Eater, joining in just like the singing of the stars.

53

When we come out of the Deep Dark, there's
a whole welcoming committee waiting for us.

The beat-up tin-can ship that is the *Hindsight* looks tiny
next to the huge, bristling-with-weaponry *Peacemaker*—
uh-oh, those are the StarLeague military leaders. What are
they doing here?—and beyond that is the sleeker, smaller,
but just as dangerous *Arrow*. There are also a bunch of other
StarLeague ships that look like troop transports—they must
be carrying all the cadets who were supposed to die as part of
the mission to fight the Eater. Off to the edges of the crowd of
ships is the *Skeleton*, which must have its crew aboard again.
And linked up with the *Arrow* is another ship. It's bigger and
more beat-up than the *Hindsight*, and looks more dangerous,
like it might be pirates.

Drigo is at the controls of the shuttle; Captain Astra leans past him to point out the front window. "That's Min Zox's ship," she tells me.

As we get closer to the fleet of ships, the blackdragon kid uncoils from around our shuttle, sings a last song of thanks to us, and fades into the darkness to rejoin the rest of the blackdragons.

All I want to do is go back home to the *Hindsight*. But my mom has a different plan.

"We're going to talk to Commander Io," she says. "And put things right."

Drigo flies our shuttle to the *Arrow*, and we link up, and the eight of us—I'm carrying the Donut-pillow—go through the hatch and along the corridors to the bridge to report in. The bridge is crowded with people—officers and others—but the first person we notice is Min Zox.

She's standing beside the command chair with her muscly arms crossed and her long tintacles braided back, looking tough and cold and strong.

Electra and Miracle stop short, staring at her.

Min Zox stares back at them.

On the shuttle, we were crowded, but Electra and Miracle wedged themselves into a corner, put their tintacly heads together, and had a quiet conversation. I didn't listen in, because it was private, between sisters, but I guess Electra told Miracle about Min Zox, their mother, and how she'd lost *both* of her daughters and it had made her cold, like ice. When we arrived at the *Arrow*, Miracle looked sort of shaky and excited to finally meet her.

"So . . ." Miracle says quietly to her sister as they stand there inside the door of the *Arrow*'s bridge. "That's her, isn't it? Our mother? She really does want us back?"

Electra nods. Her tintacles are loose, and so are Miracle's, and they are both flushing through different colors—muddy brown confusion, pink excitement, purple shyness.

"Well?" Miracle says impatiently. "Aren't we supposed to . . . you know. Go do that hugging thing?"

Electra casts me a sideways look, and when I nod encouragingly, she brightens. "Why not?" She reaches down and takes Miracle's hand, and together they walk across the shiny deck to their mother, who doesn't react.

"This is Miracle," Electra says, pointing to her sister.

"Hello," Miracle says, almost shyly.

Min Zox just stares at them, her face frozen.

My own mom is standing next to me. "Sheesh," she whispers. "Just hug each other already."

But they don't hug. Because that's not what Tintaclodians do.

Still staring at her daughters, Min Zox reaches back and loosens her long tintacles from their braid. They are muddy brown with uncertainty, just like her daughters' tintacles. Unraveling, they start to flush pink and purple and wave around Min Zox's head.

Then Electra and Min step closer, and *their* tintacles start to wave, and then the three of them lean their heads together as their tintacles do the hugging.

I'm watching her, so I see when Min Zox's face changes—icy coldness melts into tears and a smile.

And then the three of them are laughing, and their entwined tintacles turn a rainbow of joy, mother and daughters together again.

At the same time, big, pink-skinned Rose is lumbering across the metal deck and then being hugged by his even bigger tattooed father, and Drigo is holding tightly to his father, who is holding even more tightly to him, and Tyran joins his mothers, who both pat him on the head and shoulders, which is, I guess, what lizardian families do when they greet each other.

Commander Io comes to stand next to me and Captain Astra.

"You have any kids?" my mom asks her.

Commander Io's ancient, wrinkly face creases into a smile. "Maybe," she says softly, watching the kids and their parents. "Someday."

Beyond her stands a group of five important-looking StarLeague officers. The general who took over command of the *Peacemaker* is one of them. He's a very tall, very stern-looking lizardian wearing a military uniform with a star pin on the collar. He's dangerous.

Commander Io takes over. "General Gnar," she says to the *Peacemaker* commander, "the threat from the extra-galactic amorphous intelligence cluster—the blob—has ended."

General Gnar gives a sharp shake of his head. "No," he

snaps. "We are still on high alert." At his words, the rest of the StarLeague officers pull out their blasters. "A threat remains," the general goes on. And then he points, and all five of the officers aim their weapons . . .

At me.

54

Oops. Nobody knows exactly what happened when the Eater—Wow—took back the little piece of me that was the black hole. Captain Astra might not realize it either.

They still think I'm an extremely dangerous shapeshifter who could change into the Hunter and take this ship apart.

The StarLeague officers are all bristling their guns. Commander Io is protesting, but one of them takes aim, as if they're about to fire, and I feel a quick bolt of terror because I can't shapeshift my way out of this. For the first time ever, I'm a squishy, defenseless human. And then Electra, looking fierce and angry, puts herself between the soldiers and me, pulling out her own blaster and shoving me behind her, and my mom joins her, and Miracle guards my other side.

"Shift into the Hunter," Miracle hisses. "Take their weapons away."

"I can't," I say, catching my breath.

She's gripping a blaster and scowling at the StarLeague officers. She flicks a glance at me. "What?"

"I'm not a shapeshifter anymore," I tell her.

Miracle blinks. "Reeeeeeeally?"

"Really," I say. "I'm not sure how to tell everybody."

"Easy," Miracle says briskly. She lowers her weapon and steps out from behind her sister and my mom.

"Hey, *everybody*!" she shouts, and the military types aim their weapons at her. Miracle reaches over and drags me out where they can all see me. "See this kid, Trouble? He's not a weird, dangerous shapeshifter anymore. If he was, you"—she points at the StarLeague officers—"would already be disarmed, and our squad would have taken over this ship." She turns and whispers to me. "Why aren't you a shapeshifter anymore?"

"I could shift because of a tiny black hole inside me, and I gave it back to the Eater," I explain.

Miracle repeats this information loudly, and then I see my mom nodding and the StarLeague officers murmuring to each other, and there, it's done. Weapons are lowered.

"Thanks," I say to Miracle.

"You," Electra growls at her sister, "are impossible."

"I do my best," Miracle says cheerfully.

Commander Io is nodding. "Clearly," she announces, with a frown at the StarLeague commander, "we have no more reason to consider ourselves in danger or at war. According to StarLeague law, we must reorient toward our peacetime missions—colonization of planets, aid and assistance to those in need, science, and exploration."

As my mom would say, *heh*. Always good to use the StarLeague's laws against it.

The StarLeague general gives a curt nod. "We must be given proof that the blob is no longer a threat."

Commander Io glances at me. "You can provide this?"

"Yep," I say. If the StarLeague leaders want to visit Wow, well, I'm sure it'll be very curious and interested in meeting them.

Then my mom interrupts. "That," she tells Commander Io, pointing at the reunited families, "must never happen again. The StarLeague has to end the cadet training program."

Commander Io nods. "Of course. Despite the threat from the Eater, it was a terrible strategy that should never have been started." She waves a hand. "The senior cadets are already here, on troop transports. We will immediately send them back to their homes. The academy on Apex-9 will be closed, and all of the remaining cadets . . ." She pauses. "The *children* . . . will be reunited with their families."

While she's talking, Electra nods, looking happy and determined. "Good," she puts in.

Commander Io turns to her. "Will you and your sister and your squad help with that?"

Electra glances at her mother, who nods. "Yes," Electra says. "Of course."

All the cadets' parents will be so glad to see them. But it's not going to be easy. The cadets are highly trained weapons. It will be hard for them to learn how to be kids again. Commander Io says she will make sure they get the help they need to do that.

Then Commander Io starts giving orders about the troop transports and about de-weaponizing the *Peacemaker* so it can help take kids back to their homes, and it seems like she's in charge in a way she wasn't before. The military types are all agreeing, so maybe the StarLeague can go back to the way it used to be.

It won't be easy for them, either. The StarLeague has been preparing to fight the Eater for twelve years. It'll be hard for it to go back to its original purpose: exploration and helping people.

But with Commander Io leading the way, I bet they can do it. It's clear she was really good at exploration, and I wonder about all of the strange and interesting places she's been in her long life. Our galaxy is a wild and wonderful place. There's so much more out there. I have a sudden longing to see more of it. *All* of it.

I've seen so much already. From deepest space to gleaming space stations to military ships, to The Knowledge's asteroid and actual planets. And I've met so many interesting people.

It's funny how, in a huge galaxy with zillions of people and places, just one place can become home, and just a few people can become family.

Which makes it even harder to say goodbye to them.

I take a deep breath and hug Donut to my chest. Because it's time for me to say goodbye to Electra.

55

My mom is with the StarLeague officers, telling them that the StarLeague needs to hire more cargo ships. "You know," she says, "what you need is ships like the *Hindsight* and like Min Zox's ship." I know my captain. She likes sneaking around, and she likes danger, but she also likes making money, and if she can work for the StarLeague delivering supplies to people who need them, well, that's what she'll do.

I'm standing by myself with my arms wrapped around Donut.

Electra had gone to talk to her mother and Miracle, but now she leaves them and comes over to me.

"You all right, T?" she asks.

"I feel weird," I tell her, "not being a shapeshifter anymore." I look down at myself. "Do I look different?"

"No," she says. "You *seem* different."

"I am different," I admit. "But I'm still me."

She rolls her eyes. "T, you are the most *you* person I have ever met. Of course you're still you."

Feeling better, I smile at her. "Here," I say, holding out the fringed, stripy, highly decorated pillow. "I think Donut wants to be with you."

"Thank you," she says solemnly, taking it. "I will take good care of it." She pauses. "T, you know I'm not coming back to the *Hindsight* with you?"

I nod sadly. "You have to help get the kids to their homes. And you should be with your mom."

"Yes, well . . ." She glances over her shoulder at her mother and sister. "I think Miracle and I will live some of the time with her, but you're my family too."

As she says that, my human heart starts beating faster, hopeful.

"We'll live part-time on the *Hindsight*," Electra goes on, "if it's all right with Captain Astra."

"It *will* be," I say happily.

Miracle catches her eye and comes over to us. "What's going on?" she says bluntly. "You're keeping that ugly pillow?" she asks Electra.

As Electra explains about Donut, I watch them, happy that they are my friends, but already missing them.

And then it's time. I say goodbye to Commander Io and the other cadets in our squad. Electra gives me a hug, and Miracle gives me a hug that makes her tintacles turn a funny green-to-purple color that I *think* means she *might* be starting to like me. They go off to help return the cadets to their families, and then to figure out their own family. And I go home with my mom.

At home, on the *Hindsight*, I follow Captain Astra into the mess-room, feeling more tired than I've ever been in my entire life.

Reetha's at the table, and when she sees me coming in, she gets to her feet, studies me carefully, then nods.

I realize that all along Reetha saw something in me that nobody else did. "You knew, didn't you?" I ask her. "That I had a tiny black hole inside me."

Her golden eyes glitter. "You. Didn't?" she asks.

I think if she were a human, she would be laughing her head off.

Everyone else in the crew says they're glad I'm back, and we have a delicious vegetarian dinner made by Telly, and chocolate cake to celebrate, and we even get Amby and The Knowledge on the screen to join us, and then everybody goes off to bed, the captain goes to check on the bridge, and I go over and flop on the couch.

Lying there, I hold up my hand and examine it. Well, this is me. Warm-blooded human. Bones, skin, hair on my head, mouth for talking with, weird ears, feet for walking. A human kid.

The mess-room door opens and my mom comes in. Without saying anything, she goes into the galley to make herself a cup of kaff. When she comes over to the couch, she drops a pile of protein bars on my stomach.

I sit up.

"How're you doing, kiddo?" my mom asks, taking a sip of kaff. She stands there, looking down at me.

I feel . . .

"I'm not hungry," I realize, examining the pile of food she just gave me. "Actually, I may never eat another protein bar for the rest of my life."

"Hah," she says.

Being not hungry is a very good, peaceful feeling. I lean back on the couch with a tired sigh. I think it's going to be hard for me too. I was the Hunter, and now I'm not the most powerful being in the galaxy. I'm not even the most powerful person on this ship! I don't know what it's going to be like.

But I do know three things.

One, I'm not running from anything. Nobody is after me.

Two, I'm not running to anywhere. I'm already here.

Three, I'm a kid. A regular kid. I'm Trouble—and I'm the only one.